JOE GOSH

JOE GOSH
TOM DE HAVEN

ILLUSTRATED BY
RALPH REESE

A MILLENNIUM BOOK

A BYRON PREISS BOOK

WALKER AND COMPANY, NEW YORK

Cover painting by Ralph Reese.
Book design by Alex Jay/Studio J.
Book edited by David M. Harris.

Special thanks to Amy Shields.

Millennium Books and the Millennium symbol are trademarks of
Byron Preiss Visual Publications, Inc.

Library of Congress Cataloging-in-Publication Data

De Haven, Tom.
    Joe Gosh / Tom De Haven ; illustrated by Ralph Reese.
        p.   cm.—(A Millennium book)
    "A Byron Preiss book."
    Summary: Joe's life takes a humorous turn when he
encounters a scientists with a potion that can make supermen
out of ordinary "joes."
ISBN 0-8027-6824-5
[1. Science fiction. 2. Humorous stories.] I. Reese, Ralph,
ill. II. Title. III. Series.
PZ7.D33948Jo   1988   [Fic]—dc 19   88-5652

Printed in the United States of America.

This one is for Chris and Anitra.

JOE GOSH

CHAPTER

That Sunday evening, as Joe Gosh sat morosely watching television, a batch of junk mail tied with red-and-white bakery string appeared with a crackle above his set and fritzed the picture. For almost five seconds, it hung suspended in midair, then wobbled and suddenly dropped, scattering divers charity appeals, catalogs, and magazine-subscription offers across the red linoleum floor. Immediately, the TV resumed playing. On the screen, a desperate mother, pursued by a maniac from another planet, was carrying her bundled infant through a blizzard.

Getting slowly to his feet and sidling gingerly around behind the sofa as though being growled at by a Labrador retriever, Gosh waited for something further to happen—a sequel, a cataclysm. But nothing did, and at last he breathed again. Then he breathed normally. And finally, Gosh came back around the sofa, stooped and picked up a newsprint booklet from Publishers Clearing House. It felt warm and gritty. The gummed address label read: Ira Jeeters, 83 Avenue M.

That was at the north end of town, Avenue M, at least a mile away.

As he walked in slow, tight circles around the inexplicable junk mail—though some of it had been sent merely to Occupant, every sticker bore the same address—Gosh wondered if he should call his best friend, Del Forno, who was telling stories that evening at the Blue Robot, just up the block. But no, Del would only assume that Gosh, depressed unto insomnia, was now seeing things. He'd say something like, Would you please quit thinking about Vicki Zomba and just go to bed?

Gosh pulled thoughtfully at his bottom lip, glanced over at the TV—the mother was still trudging head-down against the blinding snow—and made a snap decision: he grabbed the city telephone directory. There was an Ira Jeeters listed, at the Avenue M address. Ira and Juliet Jeeters. Gosh dialed the number, and while it was ringing, tried to think of something to say first that wouldn't sound, well, stupid. Nothing came to mind. This was the craziest thing, boy.

A woman answered, and Gosh swallowed, but asked finally for Ira Jeeters.

"He can't be disturbed now. But this is Ira's sister. May I take a message?"

"You don't know me," said Gosh, "but I was watching television a minute ago, and this sounds nuts, but all of a sudden this mail appeared. Out of thin air? Addressed to Ira Jeeters. Would you happen to know anything about it?" His mouth felt dry, and his cheeks were roasting. "Hello? This isn't a crank call. I'm serious. Really."

He could hear the woman draw a breath. "Where are you?"

"On Morning Street. Eleven Morning Street."

She said nothing for several seconds. Then she asked him for his name again, and how to spell it. "Just like wow," he said, "only Gosh." Then she wanted to know his phone number.

After she'd written it all down, he said, "So what's going on?"

She said, "Can Ira call you back? He'll call you right back."

"Yeah, but I got all this mail on my floor. I don't understand."

She said, "Don't be spooked, it's only my silly brother." Then there was a soft click, followed by the dial tone.

CHAPTER

Joe Gosh was living that summer in a barracks-type building that used to be an American Legion post and ladies' auxiliary. Whenever it rained hard, he had to get out the Savarin cans, but rent was cheap—just under thirty-five grand a month—and there was plenty of space, and no other tenants—nobody downstairs or across a hall to ax the door if he played his old blues records or his Bally pinball machine at four o'clock in the morning. It had a wet bar, several urinals that wouldn't flush, and an oil portrait of General Henry Moschops mounted on the wall. In front, of course, was a flagpole, and in the side yard, an army howitzer whose muzzle was usually stuffed with chicken bones and soda cartons from the Big Boy restaurant directly across the street.

"What a dump," said Ira Jeeters. "I wouldn't live here on a bet."

He'd showed up five minutes ago, a tall and narrow-chested young man, younger even than Gosh, who was twenty. He had thinning black hair and a bad, pitted complexion—Jeeters did, not Gosh; Gosh was a husky blond who resembled the perfect municipal lifeguard—and he was wearing green fatigue pants and a pilly orange sweatshirt. On his feet were a pair of black novelty shoes, the kind that roar like a World Series crowd whenever you take a step. "I think you have some mail of mine," he'd said when Gosh had opened the front door. "You're Joe Wow?"

"Gosh. Joe Gosh."

"My sister said you told her your name was Wow."

"She misunderstood."

"How could she misunderstand a thing like that? Wow doesn't sound like Gosh, at all." He'd frowned, then turned and called outside—"Julie!"—to a slim woman in burgundy jeans and a man's white dress shirt who was leaning against the passenger door of a powder-blue Chevy. Woman and machine were both fiercely illumined by a vapor-arc streetlight. "He says his name is Gosh. You got it wrong."

She'd moved one shoulder in a kind of half-shrug.

"So what's going on here?" Gosh had asked then.

"Well, I don't know, exactly," said Jeeters, and his smile struck Gosh as a wee bit supercilious. "Can I come in?"

But as soon as he had, taking one roaring step across the saddle, he'd stopped dead in his tracks. He'd glanced down at the red floor and up at the drop ceiling, scanned the wet bar and Gosh's antique drawing table, then blinked at the picture of Moschops on the wall. He'd smiled sourly, and made that crack about not living there on a bet.

"Well, nobody's asking you to live here," said Gosh, who'd already decided he didn't like this person, not one bit.

Jeeters said, "Don't get sore. I'm lacking in the social graces—at least that's what Julie always tells me." He spotted the junk mail then, and his sleepy eyes opened wide.

"I was watching television," said Gosh, "and all of a sudden—"

"Did you do anything—adjust the set, anything like that?"

"No."

Jeeters got down slowly on one knee and picked up a solicitation from the Humane Society. He held it finically by a corner and shook it. A very fine bluish powder sprinkled off. Gosh noticed that there was a picture of a sad-eyed baby seal on the back flap. "Has it been repaired lately?"

"The set?"

"Well, what are we talking about?" said Jeeters. "Of course the set!"

"You want a punch in the mouth?"

"Sorry."

"Not officially repaired."

"What?"

"I mean," said Gosh, "I didn't bring it to a repairman or anything. But last week, the color kept going off and coming on, so this friend of mine opened up the front panel, there, and did some adjusting with that little thingamajig. I'm just watching television and your mail appears. You going to tell me how come?"

"Did you happen to check the time, when it happened?"

"No."

"You're a big help," said Jeeters, taking a clear, fold-top sandwich bag from his shirt pocket. As Gosh stood there, tapping a foot and sucking irritably on his front teeth, Jeeters brushed blue grit from piece after piece of junk mail into the plastic baggie. He sealed the zip-lock and stood up. "I can't figure this blue stuff out," he said.

"Yeah? Well, I can't figure you out."

Jeeters smiled as though he'd been paid a strong compliment. "That's what everybody says."

He'd fetched out a forty-nine-dollar disposable lighter, and now, thumbing the wheel, touched the flame to a subscription offer from the Wonder City Philharmonic Orchestra. He snorted when the envelope failed to catch fire. Then he tried to light a color catalog of outdoorsy clothes. That wouldn't burn, either. "Could I trouble you for a pair of scissors?"

"Not till you tell me what the heck's going on."

Jeeters sneered, then turned his back on Gosh and attempted to rip in half the annual plea from the local Red Cross. He struggled with it, clenching his teeth and grunting. But the little white envelope refused to be torn. Jeeters expelled his breath. "Please," he said. "A pair of scissors, in the name of science."

Gosh muttered but relented, going over and grabbing scissors from the taboret that was cater-corner with his art table.

Jeeters, in the meantime, had collected all the mail and

deposited it on top of the wet bar. "Thanks," he said, slipping the scissors awkwardly on his thumb and pointing finger; he was left-handed.

After taking a few preliminary snips at the air, Jeeters tried to cut through a catalog offering discounted classic movies-on-tape, none over a thousand dollars. And what happened, the pivot screw popped out and the cutting blades broke into chunky pieces. Jeeters laughed uproariously and did a brief jig around the barracks.

8

"You think that's funny?" said Gosh. "You know what scissors cost?"

"I'll pay for them, I'll buy you a new pair! And I'll buy the TV off you too, while I'm here. Say, five thousand bucks?"

"Get lost."

"It's used! And you already told me the color comes and goes. What, are you going to deny you ever said that now?" Jeeters stuck out his jaw belligerently, as belligerently as a jaw as recessed as his probably ever got, and Joe Gosh was tempted to take a swift poke at it. But just at that moment, there was a loud thumping noise, and the barracks door flew open.

A tan-and-white spaniel bounded in, dragging a braided leash. Toenails scrabbling on the linoleum, the dog madly dashed the full length of the place, ricocheted off the rear wall, turned around and started back toward the open doorway, where the pretty, dark-haired woman who'd been standing by the Chevy was now hunkered down.

"Bad Nippy," she said, snatching the dog's leash and giving the animal a mild chastening swat on its haunch. "I'm sorry," she said to Gosh, blushing. "I'm Julie Jeeters." Then, "Bad Nippy," she said again, tugging on the dog's leash and starting to go back outside.

The TV caught her attention, however, and she paused, frowning in its direction. "Did the mother get her baby to the hospital in time?" she asked, pointing at the screen, upon which an ad for spaghetti sauce—or was it youth creme?—was now in progress: a twinkly-eyed grandmother serving her big, happy family a real Italian meal. "Or did that psycho Venusian catch her?"

Gosh said, "I guess I kind of lost track."

"This is the second time I started watching that movie," she said. "It's a repeat. And I missed the ending both times."

"My sister is always complaining about me," said Jeeters.

"I am not!"

"Are too."

"Well," she said, "if you'd get your driver's license, maybe I could see the end of a movie from time to time."

"Always complaining," said Jeeters.

"I don't *mind* driving you everyplace, Ira. I just think you could get your own license."

"I will! And then I'll never bother you again."

The sister looked shyly at Gosh. "He won't ever learn to drive."

"I will!" said Jeeters. "You'll see. I'll go get my learner's permit tomorrow. And I'll never bother you again. You can sit in front of your dopey TV set for the rest of your life, see if I care."

Gosh said, "Is anybody going to let me know what's going on? Or am I supposed to guess?"

Jeeters shrugged. "You have anything to eat?" he said. "Like a donut or something?"

CHAPTER

"This was all our father's idea. So to speak. He used to be a mailman."

Jeeters was talking with his mouth full of a chocolate graham cracker. Gosh had been surprised to discover a package of them stuck way, way back in his refrigerator, behind a jar of red peppers. He hadn't remembered buying chocolate grahams. Possibly, he'd decided, Del Forno had brought them over one evening. Del was always dropping by to practice his stories, and if there was one thing that Del liked—besides the sound of his own voice telling lies, of course—it was sweets, particularly milk chocolate.

"Our father," said Jeeters, "delivered mail for almost twenty years. And boy! did he get sick of that. He used to say what I should do, I should find a better way. So I've been fooling around, the last couple of months, trying to come up with a matter transmitter. To deliver the mail."

Gosh cocked his head. They were all sitting around his little Formica-topped kitchen table, Gosh, Jeeters, and Jeeters's sister, Julie. "I thought we were going to get our mail by computer, in a couple of years. It's what I read."

Jeeters made a dismissive face. "Never happen," he said. "People don't want to turn on their computers and get electronic mail. They want the real thing." He held up both hands and shook them, like a Fundamentalist minister gesticulating about heaven or hell. "They want *mail*." He helped himself to another graham cracker. "They want to rip envelopes."

Julie Jeeters hadn't eaten any crackers herself. She'd taken one from the package, but then had broken it up and was now feeding it, bit by bit, to her dog. Nippy lay at her feet, well behaved now.

"It's called the Jeeter Jiffy," said Jeeters. "I dropped the 's' for a more euphonius sound. For a snappier brand name."

Gosh said, "What are you talking about?"

"Man oh Manischewitz, don't you listen good, Mr. Wow? I'm talking about my transmitter—the Jeeter Jiffy. I put the mail in here and it comes out there. It's all done with magnets."

"It comes out *where*? Over my television set?"

Jeeters flushed, offended. "I built a receiver—there's a receiver in my workshop—except, at the moment, it doesn't appear to be working so great." He twisted his lips to one side, nodded at the junk mail still piled on the wet bar, and said, "I don't know *how* all that stuff ended up *here*."

Julie Jeeters laughed. "On Monday?" she said. "Ira put a copy of *TV Guide* in his goofy machine and it wound up under the pulpit light at St. John's Espiscopal Church. During a funeral."

"These things happen," said Jeeters, unabashed. He smiled at Gosh.

"Ira's always inventing things," said Julie. "He has patents on several bacteria."

Gosh nodded, and crossed one leg over the other. Then he sat back and, taking a fiber-tip pen from his shirt, started doodling on his pants leg. He was wearing beige jeans, and what he doodled on them were little cartoony dinosaurs—a diplodocus, a nothosaurus, a bronto, then a pteranodon. He always doodled when he was nervous or was at a loss for something to say. The only sound was the spaniel licking its chops.

"So how come the mail didn't burn?" Gosh finally asked. It had been on his mind for the past half hour. "How come—my scissors broke?"

Jeeters shrugged his narrow shoulders. "Isn't that something? I have no idea."

Julie was looking at her hands in her lap. "Lots of times Ira's experiments turn out a little funny."

"The history of science," said Jeeters, "is full of happy accidents."

"And some not so happy." Julie looked up at Gosh. "Ira went to this special high school, for the biggest brains? And he did something to a computer, and you know what? All of a sudden, they had this, I guess, demon running around the dormitory. What was its name, Ira?"

"Nobody could pronounce it." Jeeters sat there and scowled. He'd folded his arms across his chest.

"They kicked Ira out. It was really too bad. He had a scholarship and all."

Gosh said, "So what're you doing, you're working for the Postal Service?"

"I don't work for anybody!" Ira said. "When the Jiffy is done, I get a patent, I make a trillion dollars. But first I got to build a receiver that *receives*. A mailbox that *works*. You can't have mail being delivered to the wrong address. That defeats the whole purpose."

"Ira's going to be a trillionaire before he's nineteen—that's his goal." Julie kissed melted chocolate from her fingertips, and for some strange reason that simple action caused Gosh to feel prickly and to blush. "Now that billionaires are a dime a dozen."

Suddenly, Jeeters grabbed another handful of graham crackers, stuffed them into his pants pockets, and stood up from the table. "Well, thanks again for calling us about the mail. That was pretty smart of you—I mean, to look at the name on the labels." The way that he said *smart*, wrapping his shiny lips around the word, and widening his eyes, it was clear to Gosh that Ira Jeeters didn't think that anybody, besides himself, had too much going on upstairs.

Jeeters wiped his hands on his sweatshirt, then took out his wallet, which bore on its surface a perishing decal of somebody sober-looking and with a long beard—possibly Alexander Graham Bell. He slid out his Only-U card, a gold one.

"You want to get your press, we'll do a little business. Seventy-five hundred bucks for the TV. That's fair."

"Wait a second," said Gosh. "Why do you need my set?"

Julie said, "No receiver, no trillion dollars. He tried to buy the pulpit at St. John's. He even tried to buy the *casket,* just in case."

"Well, I'm not selling him my TV. At least, not for a lousy seventy-five hundred dollars."

Jeeters glared, then, with an explosive sigh, agreed to double it. "Fifteen thousand dollars! And that's my final offer. Now get your press."

Gosh smiled slightly, and as he ran a sales slip through his credit-card press, he was still thinking about that invulnerable mail. How it wouldn't burn, how you couldn't cut it. Pretty neat. This probably all had something to do with space and time, space warps, other dimensions, and stuff like that. He'd seen a lot of movies about cool stuff like that.

"Julie," said Jeeters, "I'll get Nippy if you'll take care of the TV."

She obliged, unplugging it, picking it up, and, with a bashful parting smile at Gosh, carting it away. Jeeters, without so much as a good-bye, followed with the dog. His shoes cheered uproariously.

Gosh put away the press and drew an allosaurus.

CHAPTER

Del Forno was telling that one about the time X. S. Powers came to the orphanage on Founder's Day.

"By then he was almost sixty years old," said Del, "and far from being in his prime. It used to be, he'd do a personal appearance, he'd bring along a shotgun, let somebody fire it at his head. Now it was a BB rifle. But still, it was kind of great to see him."

As he talked, Del's hands gestured frenetically. In the blue spotlight, his skin looked unhealthy, glistening with perspiration. Occasionally, clouds of safe smoke would waft his way. These were actually projections from the control booth at the rear of the premises, a noncarcinogenic light show. After the prohibition of tobacco last year, it was discovered that nightclub patrons became desultory, or, even worse, bloodthirsty and violent without periodic bursts throughout the evening of gray-blue cigarette smoke.

"... so, like, he does his regular spiel, the same old twenty-five-thousand dollar lecture, telling everybody what we already knew—all that stuff about him being a test pilot flying over Utah and breaking some barrier, who knows which, and coming out the other side of the world, over Thailand or someplace, and his plane breaking up into a zillion little pieces and him landing on the ground, in some village, on his feet, not a parachute, not a scratch. And then, for about half an hour? X. S. showed these color slides—him flying away with an oil tanker that was going down in Hurricane Dinah, him catching a bunch of political bank robbers with a flick of his pinky, then holding up some bridge on the Governor Moschops Thruway, all that kind of stuff. And then, then he let this fourth-grade kid shoot him with BB's. But he said, 'Aim at my chest, son, okay? Right about here.' " Del pointed to his sternum.

Joe Gosh had heard Del's version of this story perhaps three dozen times before, and was paying hardly any attention to it now. He sat at the bar drinking Fiz and thinking about Vicki Zomba. No-Deposit whirred by, checked Gosh's glass, and finding it empty, gave him a refill. Then it produced a damp cloth and wiped away bar spill.

No-Deposit was one of Del Forno's half-dozen burnished blue robots, seven feet tall on wheels, assembled from a Tandy kit. Since this particular model's physique was vaguely reminiscent of a classic cola bottle, Del had customized it with tiny circles meant to be read as carbonation bubbles. However, the effect more closely resembled a sort of smallpox.

"Anyhow," Del Forno was saying now, "before he left—he had to appear that same night in Wisconsin, at the Sells-Floto Circus—he said that anybody who wanted to ride on his shoulders, could. Free of charge. So I got on line. I'm twelve years old, and I get on line, all right? To wait my turn. I was never a pushy kind of kid, though, so where was I, but dead last. But at least I was on line. I'm on line for a free ride! First kid goes up, gives X. S. Powers a ticket, and off they go. Flying over the orphanage, the kid hanging on, screaming with glee. I tell you, I couldn't wait. I couldn't wait to fly."

Del pulled out a handkerchief and mopped his face. He was short and round, and, as usual, he wore his clothes, a pink shirt and red pants, at least one size too small. His hair was white. It had been white for as long as Gosh had known him. They'd met at the Wonder City Home for Boys seven years ago, a year after the event that Del was talking about now.

Del hadn't been there that day to see X. S. Powers; when X. S. Powers came to the orphanage, Del Forno hadn't even been an *orphan* yet, for crying out loud. This story about waiting to go take a free ride on the superman's shoulders? It wasn't Del's story at all, it was Gosh's. Gosh had been that twelve-year-old kid waiting on line.

Del was a chronic liar who'd happily found in nightclub work an acceptable outlet for his fabrications, and now was thriving. He owned the Blue Robot, lock, stock, and automatons. Robots waited tables, worked the sound system, bounced riffraff. Even laughed at his jokes when the patrons were stiffs.

"So, now there's one more kid ahead of me," Del said. "He climbs on Powers's back, and Powers kind of . . . lurches. And he's breathing heavy, too. But up he flies anyhow, and they're flying around and around, him and the kid, when suddenly— X. S. Powers goes into a fricken nosedive. But just before he crashes—into the goalpost on the football field—he comes out of it, and lands safe. The kid slides off his back, crying bloody murder. What happened, right? What's the matter? The matter was," said Del, opening his eyes in stagy astonishment, "the *matter* was that X. S. Powers was having a heart attack! Right there in front of us orphans. The most powerful man in the universe is going down with cardiac arrest. Plop! It's my turn in the air, but the guy is turning blue!" Del wagged his head in a slow, histrionic gesture of frustration and heartbreak.

"Well, they took him to Beth-Israel, but couldn't do much. He needed surgery, right? But they can't open him up—he's, like, *invulnerable!* Scalpels breaking left and right. So that was the end of X. S. Powers. Poor him. But hey, what about me? Poor me, too! Pity the poor little orphan boy. Pity Del Forno!"

Gosh rolled his eyes, then, because he'd heard this story *so* often—he silently mouthed Del's windup along with Del: "That's the story of my life. That could even be the title of my autobiography: *No Free Rides.*"

There were some muted chuckles.

"Thank you," Del said, "and good night." Now there was a polite smattering of applause. It was Monday, and the club was about two-thirds empty.

Wiping his face again, Del plopped down on a stool next to Gosh. "How long?" he asked.

Gosh glanced at his watch. "Seventeen minutes plus."

17

Del pursed his mouth. Sometimes the story ran only eight or nine minutes, other times as long as twenty-five. Del was of the opinion that he told it best when he kept it around twelve. He puffed his cheeks and popped his lips, then sipped at the glass of lemon-lime Kik that No-Deposit had put down in front of him.

"I stiffed tonight, didn't I?" he asked Gosh. "I really, really stiffed up there."

"You weren't bad."

"I should retire that story. I told it too much." That was a funny thing about Del. On stage he was Mr. Confidence. Off-stage, though, he was as insecure as a first-grader. "I don't think I should tell that story anymore. What do you think, Joey?"

"Maybe you shouldn't."

Del took that like a slap to the face. He even flinched. "Hey, you don't know what you're talking about, it's one of my best stories," he said. "I think you're wrong."

Gosh had been friends with Del long enough to know that now was the time to just shut up and drink his Fiz.

"You know," said Del, changing the subject, a critical tone entering his voice, "I been thinking. And I think you made a big mistake, letting that guy have your TV for only fifteen thousand."

Earlier, Gosh had told Del Forno all about last evening's screwy business.

"I got it at a yard sale. It cost me only eleven hundred bucks."

"That's not the point. If that guy's who I think he is. You said Jeeters."

Gosh nodded.

"His father was a mailman?"

Gosh nodded again.

"You should've held him up for, like, twenty-five thousand. At least."

"Right."

Over on stage, a tall man with a shock of orange hair that looked like stony coral was adjusting the microphone.

"I'm serious, Joey. That guy's father—the mailman? Is a multibillionaire. He won the lottery last year. You've seen his face on billboards. In the subway? Nineteen billion dollars."

Gosh felt sick to his stomach. But that lasted for only a second. "Well, the set wasn't worth twenty-five thousand," he said.

Del Forno laughed, meaning: Gosh, you're flaky. "So what was the sister like?"

"All right. Kind of shy."

"Do you think she'd go out with me?"

Gosh made a face. Del Forno was a washout with the opposite sex. Half the stories that he told at the club were about his disastrous dates, though heavily embroidered.

"She pretty?"

"I guess. Yeah."

"Put in a good word for me, next time you see her."

"I don't expect to see her again."

"Or *don't* tell her about me, what a great guy I am," said Del. "Go out with her yourself."

The guy on stage—he called himself Bud Polyp—was tuning his guitar.

"I don't want to go out with her," said Gosh.

"Her father won nineteen billion dollars."

"So you told me."

Bud Polyp's first number was a pretty ballad called "Order Diptera," about mosquitoes, about two mosquitoes in love. Pretty controversial stuff.

"If that business had happened to *me* last night, I would've asked the sister for a date. I would've asked her to *marry* me, for crying out loud. But nothing cool like that ever happens to yours truly." He made a low mouth-noise of disgust and self-pity, then finished drinking his Kik.

Bud Polyp's next song—he said it was available on CD and digital tape, and that he'd be happy to sell a copy to anybody, and autograph the label, right after his perform-ance—was called "A Pimple Is a Small Solid Elevation of the Skin." He closed his eyes while he sang, and his lips seemed to brush the sponge that covered the mike. "A pimple is a small solid elevation of the skin. No way out," he sang, "no way in."

"I think you should call her up. This Jeeters girl. She's pretty, she's shy, she's rich—what else could you want? Don't answer."

Gosh scowled.

"Oh, forget Vicki Zomba, why don't you? Would you, please? You'll get yourself killed, Joey, making such a big pest of yourself.

"I can't help it."

"You'll be sorry."

"I'm *already* sorry."

Gosh folded his arms on the bar, then leaned down and pressed his forehead against a wristbone, thinking Vicki Zomba, Vicki Zomba.

Meanwhile, Bud Polyp was singing, "A person is a big solid elevation of a cell. Ain't it great, aren't we swell . . ."

CHAPTER 5

After the Blue Robot closed at three-fifteen, Del Forno invited Gosh to stick around and watch him play poker with No-Deposit. It was to be a grudge match, Del's grudge, since the automaton had won nearly forty-four thousand dollars from Del last Saturday. "Stay, why don't you," said Del. "You can stand behind No-D with a mirror. I'd appreciate it."

Gosh smiled but declined. "I'm going home to work," he said. By work, he meant draw another dinosaur, maybe a dilophosaurus, with colored pens. It was vaguely in the back of Gosh's mind that, one of these days, he'd put all his dinosaur sketches together, have them printed on fairly good stock, and see if the zoo shop might take them, on consignment. Or maybe he'd try to sell them as a book. Or maybe . . . "Good night, Del."

Chin in hand, Del watched Gosh head for the door. "Julie Jeeters's father," he said, "won nineteen billion dollars, buddy." Then he glared at No-Deposit across the bar and said, "Fresh deck. My deal. And no funny business."

Outside, Gosh changed his mind and, instead of walking home, took the footbridge over the Bedlam Turnpike, then strolled around that part of Wonder City called Good Neighborhood.

This was actually more than a single neighborhood, since it was slightly bigger than a square mile in size and encompassed several voting districts. Good Neighborhood was, however, unified by the tax bracket of its inhabitants, which was high, though not the highest, and by its residential architecture, which the realty people, years ago, had dubbed "heroic contempo"—granite needles that tapered and tapered and finally disappeared in the smutch.

When Gosh was a kid living at the orphanage, he'd often daydreamed of one day owning a cube-with-a-window high up in one of those dizzy-making needles. He'd stare at a CRT screen thronged with eighth-grade math problems, ninth-grade theorems, tenth-grade Shakespeare and think, I'll grow up, become a lawyer, live in a needle—have a New Year's Eve party every year.

But somewhere around his fifteenth birthday, he'd realized that he didn't *want* to become a lawyer, or a lawyer-broker, or a broker-chemist, or a chemist-entrepreneur, or anything else with the salary and perks necessary to get himself out of the Retro District and over the Bedlam Pike on a permanent basis. He didn't want to be a lawyer, he wanted to be—well, he just didn't know. And still didn't.

Unless it counted as a career to be Vicki Zomba's one great love.

One of these days he really was going to have to buckle down and think seriously about the future. One of these days.

The main thoroughfare in Good Neighborhood was Surety Boulevard, and Gosh strolled that practically from one end to the other. Since it was a weeknight, he passed very few people—an occasional giggling couple, the sporadic lurker-behind-an-elm, a barefoot man in shorty pajamas who strolled dejectedly past the oxygen reservoir, mumbling to himself about junk bonds. The curbsides were lined with ritzy cars.

At every corner, Gosh peered down the cross street, looking for one whose vapor lamps were suspiciously dark. At last he found one, Betty Street, and, tingling with excitement, turned down it. As he walked, very slowly now, he examined every parked car that he passed, paying special attention to Cadillacs, Ma Zomba's bait of choice. He'd gone all the way down one side of the street, crossed at the corner, and was working his way toward Surety again when he spotted a car he thought might be It. A brand-new Caddy Caudillo.

Fetching out a penlight—Gosh always carried a penlight,

as well as an ear button crammed with every song that Robert Johnson had ever recorded in his short, sad life, a subway token, and a cloudy chunk of quartz; fetching out his penlight, he used it to scour the Caddy's deep padded dash.

He grinned when he spotted the world's finest, absolutely finest, car stereo system. What thief could resist *that*?

Then Gosh laughed out loud when he saw the altar.

It consisted of several pigeon feathers, an antacid tablet, a one-serving juice can with a constellation of puncture holes in the side, a key blank, an antique transistor radio, and five stuffed-animal eyes, everything dumped on a fluted paper plate.

2 3

Nodding with satisfaction, Gosh used an elbow to break the driver's window.

Naturally, there was no alarm.

Come into my web, said the spider to the fly.

He popped the lock button, opened the door, brushed the seat clean of safety glass, then climbed in under the wheel.

The key, of course, was in the ignition.

There was nothing to do now except to wait.

He didn't have to wait long. No more than half a minute.

His head began to grow heavy, and a sort of percolation started behind his eyeballs, then gradually moved down his neck, then all the way down his spine. His mouth turned sticky.

Although he'd been through this twice before, still Gosh felt a pang of sheer terror when he tried to scratch an itch on the bridge of his nose and realized that he no longer had control of his body—that he couldn't lift a hand.

The dial on the cheap transistor radio lit up.

Two minutes later, Gosh was motoring out of Good Neighborhood, zipping onto the Bedlam Pike at Exit 9, heading south.

But until he steered the Caddy into a slummy garage somewhere in the Lowest East Side of Wonder City, Gosh wasn't cognizant of anything, except for his own heart beating like hip-hop in his ears. He'd driven several miles in a trance.

Then he heard a loud metallic *thunk,* and suddenly he was being pulled, roughly, from behind the steering wheel.

CHAPTER

Gosh landed on his right shoulder, on a hard cement floor that reeked of motor oil and gasoline.

The blue haze receded and his vision clarified, and then he was staring up into the ugly, the angry, face of Ma Zomba. The peculiar birthmarks on her temples—they looked like soil worms, three to a temple—throbbed and darkened. Her teeth were bared, and clenched.

Gosh tried a smile, but that only got him a swift kick between two ribs. Ma wore ballet slippers, with lead in the toes.

Over the garage's loudspeaker system, the Honky Tonk Man was singing "Crazy Arms."

The Queen of Crime said, "I should put you back in that car and just let you drive off some pier."

Gosh said nothing in reply, but scrambled to his feet when she ordered him to. Two of her zombies, who appeared to be identical twins, though each dressed differently and sported different facial scars, stood nearby, their expressions blank, their machine guns leveled at Gosh's midriff.

Behind them, other zombies went dully about their criminal activities, some loading a convoy-style truck with cartons stenciled GOVERNMENT PROPERTY, others, at a trestle table, sticking phony tax stamps on packages of chewing gum, caching filter-tipped cigarettes in hollowed-out psalm books, or assembling military rifles. Another zombie, stationed at another, smaller table heaped with bracelets and brooches, had a jeweler's loupe in his left eye. His right eye never blinked.

Gosh skipped his gaze here and there, till finally he saw, curled up on a foam sofa in the corner, by an old-fangled gasoline pump—the beautiful, the breathtaking Vicki Zomba! She had on a pair of cushioned headphones and was wriggling her toes to the tempo of a song only she could hear. Or maybe she was wriggling her toes at Gosh, in a sort of cute greeting. His heart leapt.

"You're becoming the worst sort of pest," said Ma Zomba. "I really should just get rid of you." And Gosh, distracted by Vicki, nearly shrugged. He caught himself in time, thank goodness. Ma Zomba was quite capable of doing whatever she threatened, without batting an eyelash.

Gosh said, "I wanted to see Vicki again. I didn't know how else to find her. I mean—you move your hideout almost every day. That doesn't make my life easy."

Then he burlesqued a big gulp, trying to be charming, but Ma just glared, and knocked him in the shoulder with the heel of her hand. Her black dress swished when she moved, and squirts of current appeared in each shoulder pad, then wriggled down the sleeves and exited at the cuffs like startled snakes. It was an electric dress, several years out of style, not that Ma cared two figs for things like fashion.

"I don't want her seeing you. You seeing her. She knows that. You're not her type."

"Well, I can't agree, Ma." Gosh was really pushing it. "What's so wrong about me?"

"I don't like you. That's what."

Vicki had removed her headphones and was strolling barefooted across the garage floor, smiling in vast amusement. She was wearing a khaki romper, and her long legs were golden from a recent commercial tanning. She had a tumble of light-brown hair that bounced, and the reddest lips in Wonder City. Her eyes were blue, but the left one was bluer than the right. To Gosh, the most perfect of flaws!

She gave him a mildly scolding look, then burst out laughing.

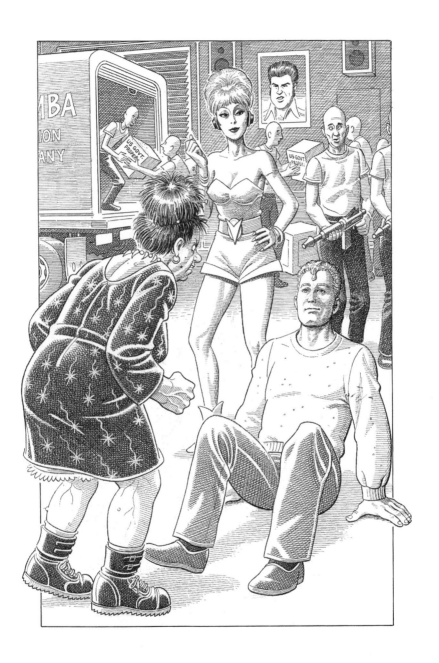

"I don't see what's so funny," snapped her mother. "I put that car on the street to catch a professional, somebody I could use—and what do I get? This . . . creature."

Gosh felt himself blush.

"Well, you have to admit," said Vicki, "he's resourceful."

Ma puffed out her lips, then glanced at the Caddy, where already one of her zombies was reglazing the broken window. He was about Gosh's age, a ponytailed skinny-belink with a variety of common tattoos on the backs of his hands, and one hoop earring.

Gosh turned slightly away from Ma, smiled at Vicki, cleared his throat, then boldly asked her if she felt like going out. Right now. For a cup of coffee, or something.

And the next thing he knew, his teeth clacked together and he was back on the floor, sitting on his butt.

"You think you're funny?" Current was going crazy now in the sleeves of Ma's dress.

"No, ma'am."

"Next time you show up here, you *stay* a zombie—understand? And I'll have you hijacking every truck from here to California. Stay away from my daughter! She's not interested in a big nobody like you!"

Ma strode over to her desk, alongside a mechanic's work-pit. She threw herself down in a swivel chair. The telephone was a plastic replica of the Honky Tonk Man, and there was also a plaster bust of him on the green blotter. There were Honky Tonk Man action figures ranged along the perimeter of the in/out basket, which was laden with chicken bones and little juice cans. Behind the desk, the cinder block wall was covered with huge color posters of his nibs—black hair gleaming, top lip curled into a sneer. Ma Zomba was the Honky Tonk Man's greatest fan. She was president of his International Fan Club, one of her few legitimate enterprises.

Vicki smiled sweetly at Gosh, then, once more, said to her mother, "But you have to admit he *is* resourceful."

"Pulling the same stunt three times, that's resourceful? I

give pretty boy one minute to get out of here," said Ma. "And he best not come looking for you again. The big nobody!"

Though discouraged, Gosh knew enough about things not to take Ma Zomba's exorbitant disdain all that personally. The fact was, she held every man on Earth in utter disdain. Except, of course, the Honky Tonk Man.

Ma still clung to the ephemeral hope that one day, one fine day he might actually reappear. But what chance was there of that? In Gosh's opinion, none. Come on, already, the Honky Tonk man had been missing almost *twenty years*—he'd been in Brazil, filming yet another one of his boneheaded movies, when he'd simply wandered off into the monkey jungle between takes, and vanished. Nineteen years ago! Did Ma really believe he was still alive? It was crazy—but then, so was Ma.

Under her watchful eye, Gosh shuffled slowly toward the garage door, which rose with a hydraulic whine as he approached. Working the control box was a zombie that Gosh vaguely recognized; probably somebody he'd seen once or twice at the Blue Robot. His lips were twitchy, and his eyeballs looked varnished.

Gosh stood in the open doorway and stared back into the garage. Vicki hesitated, then crossed the floor to see him out, causing Ma to jump to her feet, dress blazing with faddish electricity. She said, "Victoria!" and Vicki stopped cold, several feet away from Gosh.

He said, "What can I do to make her like me?"

Vicki shrugged. "Can you sing rhythm and blues?"

"Besides that."

"Listen, Gosh," she said, throwing a glance over her shoulder at Ma. "I think you're just wasting your time. I'm not even so nuts about you."

"Don't say that!"

"Well, it's true. You're nice-looking and all, but you *are* sort of a nobody—you have to admit. What are your prospects in life?" Then she laughed, kissed her fingertips and blew on them, as though dispelling dandelion fluff.

29

Gosh turned and slumped outside, and as the garage door descended, he crouched, getting one final glimpse of Vicki Zomba as she readjusted her stereo headphones.

Plunged into the deepest gloom, he started for home, kicking big chunks of broken-bottle glass ahead of him.

"Oh, Squirrely, don't be so sad. We all love you here in Wonderland!"

"Nobody loves me," said Squirrely, its corduroy hands covering its black button eyes. "If everybody loves me, how come nobody gave me a birthday party?"

"Well," said Vicki Zomba as Lady Sunny-Weather, "your birthday isn't over *yet.*" She turned and winked broadly at the audience at home, and Joe Gosh, staring at the TV set from behind his drawing table, suddenly found it difficult to breathe.

This had happened six months ago.

Gosh was in the habit of watching quiz shows in the morning while he drew—it was fun to hear a contestant's biography summed up in less than ten seconds—sergeant in the army, married, two kids—and he enjoyed the game buzzers and the breathless responses, even the commercials for bran cereals and decaffeinated coffee.

But that day—it was a Tuesday in mid-January—the regular daytime programming had been preempted on all the broadcast and cable networks because there'd been a major nuclear accident, or a new war had broken out, or something like that. Something along those lines. Gosh simply couldn't draw dinosaurs and listen to bad news at the same time, so he'd flipped through the dial, till he came to a children's show on CATV. *Baron Mencken's Wonderland.* It looked pretty dreadful, but he'd needed background noise, so he left it on and sat down.

Then Squirrely the hand puppet had appeared in a papier-mâché tree, weeping.

Then Lady Sunny-Weather had consoled him.

Then she'd turned and winked at the boys and girls at home, and Joe Gosh fell in love.

For the rest of the show, he'd stared at the screen as though hypnotized, his green felt-tip pen bleeding through an archaeopteryx.

King Candor of Wonderland threw a surprise birthday party for Squirrely, and Squirrely learned a useful lesson: Be patient.

Then Baron Mencken fed his goldfish, and demonstrated the art of tying a shoelace while singing a tuneless little ditty.

Besides Lady Sunny-Weather, the baron was the only nonpuppet on the program. He was a big bearish man who dressed more like a savings-and-loan officer than a nobleman. "Be good boys and girls," he said, "and stay out of mischief."

When the credits finally—finally!—had rolled, Gosh jotted down Vicki Zomba's name, and the name of the television production company, which happily was a local one. When he called the company, though, a prerecorded message informed him that the number was no longer in service.

So then he'd phoned the television station, Channel K, and was told that *Baron Mencken's Wonderland* was in reruns, that the show he'd just seen had been produced almost two years ago.

Gosh began tuning in to *Wonderland* every day, just to see Lady Sunny-Weather. He dreamed of her at night. In his dreams, more often than not, Gosh was a hand puppet, himself. But, no matter, they were great dreams. He had to meet her! He just had to meet the actress who played Lady Sunny-Weather. But how? How?

Then one afternoon, he saw her photograph in the daily newspaper. Her face leapt out at him from page 3. In the picture she was standing alongside a stout, angry-looking woman with large, piercing eyes.

The headline above read:

QUEEN & PRINCESS OF CRIME
NABBED IN MEGA $ SUPER-SCHEME

Gosh felt as though he'd been hit with a construction derrick. There must be some mistake! According to the story, Vicki's mother was an underworld genius, the brains behind everything—well, almost everything—crooked in Wonder City. The pair of them faced prison terms totaling more than ten thousand years.

Gosh had stayed numb for the rest of that day, and on the morning following, had showed up at the Hall of Justice, where Vicki and Ma Zomba were facing arraignment. There must've been almost a hundred picketers—LET 'EM GO!!—shuffling up and down with strange, glassy, fixed expressions in front of the colonnaded building. Gosh had scarcely been able to squeeze through the crush and get inside, where, for the very first time, he laid eyes upon the object of his desire in person.

Vicki had been dressed as Lady Sunny-Weather, in a blue gown with vibrantly colored hand-painted flowers up the front.

She stood beside her mother at the defendants' table. Ma wore a black business suit, and around her neck hung a chain of small bones, perhaps pinky or toe bones, from which dangled bottle caps, a few key blanks, some memory chips, a tiny portrait of the Honky Tonk Man encased in lucite, and several jingle bells.

While Gosh waited for the proceedings to begin, he'd scanned the spectators' gallery, and was quite surprised to observe, slumped on a bench across the aisle, Baron Mencken himself. He looked very distraught, very disheveled, and was unshaven. His eyes seemed unnaturally bright and faraway.

Gosh would never have recognized the baron at all, if he hadn't had Squirrely sheathed on his left hand and King Candor on his right.

At last, the judge appeared, and things got going.

The district attorney—or somebody like that; Gosh was too busy ogling Vicki Zomba again to pay all that much attention to who was who—began to recite a litany of the

Zombas' transgressions. Pacing the front of the courtroom and slapping the plaintiff's table for emphasis, he ticked off grand larceny, extortion, and racketeering. But then, as he pivoted around to gesture accusingly at Ma Zomba, his face paled and he began to stammer. He blinked rapidly. Then he touched his forehead, and, glancing out toward the spectators, his jaw dropped. He looked positively appalled to find himself the center of everyone's attention. He flushed, then hemmed and hawed, no longer making a bit of sense.

3 4   The judge ordered him to the bench.

There, they conferred briefly, the judge doing most of the whispering, the district attorney (or whoever) mopping his face with a silk handkerchief.

Then the judge summoned up the Zombas' attorney, and Ma accompanied him, unbidden. The judge seemed astounded by her presumptuousness, and was about to light into her when, all of a sudden, his mouth clamped shut and he just stared dumbly at Ma's necklace of miscellany.

Then everybody in court jumped in their seats when the judge struck his gavel and dismissed all the charges against both defendants.

Pandemonium ensued as news reporters scrambled for the doors, and Ma Zomba's disreputable-looking partisans cheered and whooped and hollered. Baron Mencken openly wept into his puppeted hands.

Gosh tried elbowing his way toward the defendants' table, but was only flung about like a rag doll. He finally jumped back into the gallery, then crawled on his stomach underneath the benches. He came up for air directly in back of Vicki Zomba. They were separated only by the blondwood guardrail.

Ma was still over at the judge's bench, speaking with her lawyer. She had a big sneer on her face. The district attorney (or whoever) was loitering sheepishly between the stenographer's desk and the flagpole, looking as if he'd like to join their conversation but was too polite and shy to interrupt. The judge had disappeared.

Gosh rose slowly from a crouch, and, summoning nerve, tapped Vicki on the shoulder. She flinched, and half turned around. Seeing Gosh, she widened her eyes. Then she cocked her head inquiringly.

Gosh touched a silencing finger to his lips and, with his free hand, beckoned Vicki to lean closer, to lean over the railing, so that he might whisper what he had to say.

But in a normal speaking voice, making no effort whatsoever to be quiet or conspiratorial, she asked, "Who the heck are you? You a reporter?"

Gosh froze.

Ma Zomba glanced their way, her necklace jangling, her shoulders drawing back in anger.

Gosh blurted to Vicki, "I think you're wonderful! I think you're fabulous!"

Vicki Zomba's red lips separated in surprise. "What do you want?" she said harshly. "You want my autograph?"

"No," said Gosh, then quickly added, "Well, sure, I'll take your autograph, but I'd rather marry you."

Vicki doubled over and laughed in peals. Unlike her television laughter, which always sounded synthetic and forced, this was the real thing.

"Well, I don't mean *today*," Gosh said, his chest going tight.

Then it wasn't so much his chest that felt constricted as his larynx: Ma Zomba had snatched him by the throat and was lifting him into the air. His feet kicked and pedaled helplessly.

Abruptly, she let go, and he dropped hard, whacking one wrist and the opposite elbow on the railing.

From his awkward sprawl, he gaped up to see both Vicki and Ma Zomba peering down at him.

Vicki looked bemused, possibly sympathetic.

Ma's eyes glinted with malevolence, and her big body shook.

"By some chance," she asked, "are you curious to know what it feels like to be dead?"

She touched her necklace of bones and whatnot, and Gosh was suddenly transfixed, staring at jingle bells and bits of printed circuitry.

Then his heart stopped.

Then—ten seconds later? two minutes? five minutes?—he was sitting on a bench in the spectators' gallery, mechanically punching himself over and over in the chin with his right hand. His teeth rattled and his brainpan jumped, and the court stenographer—a tall, thin man with a head of white hair—was staring at him in pop-eyed wonder.

Gosh kept hitting himself until somebody came and grabbed his arm and held it.

Even then, his arm struggled to fling itself free, and his fist remained a tight bludgeon.

His teeth felt loose.

Luckily, though, the impulse to beat himself senseless abruptly stopped. He lifted the offending hand, fingers splayed now, fingers tingling, and gingerly touched his jaw.

He winced.

Then he wiped away some bits of white froth that had collected at the corners of his mouth.

"You're going to have a nasty bruise," said Squirrely.

"I'd like to banish that witch, if I could," said King Candor.

Baron Mencken, looking sad and forlorn, sat on the bench next to Gosh.

The stenographer was carrying his machine through a doorway into the judge's chambers. The courtroom was empty.

Baron Mencken sighed loudly. Then he peeled the puppets off his hands, folded them together like a pair of socks, and stuffed them into his coat pocket. "You should never, never stare at that woman's necklace," he said, helping Gosh to his feet.

Gosh was astonished when his legs nearly crumpled under him.

"Believe me," said the baron, "I speak from experience."

He walked Gosh out into the lobby of the Hall of Justice.

"What do you mean, from experience?"

"Do you know who I am?"

"Yes."

"Ever seen my show?"

"All the time."

"What did you think of Lady Sunny-Weather?"

Gosh had been momentarily at a loss for words. Lady Sunny-Weather? Why, she was, she was—

"The world's worst actress, right? Believe me, it wasn't *my* idea to give her that job. But whatever Mother wants," the baron had added, rolling his glazed eyes, "Mother gets."

"Where'd they go?"

The baron had shrugged.

"How can I find them again?"

"Steal a Cadillac with a Goldspeke stereo system."

Gosh had blinked. "What?"

And Baron Mencken, sliding his Only-U card into a lottery vending machine on the street corner, said. "Be a good boy, why don't you, and stay out of mischief."

Six months ago.

CHAPTER

Gosh was noodling around with a hypsilophodon when Julie Jeeters came by with his television set.

After getting home from Ma Zomba's latest hideout, he'd had a rough time falling asleep. He'd tossed and turned the better part of an hour, then flung himself out of bed to go watch some TV. When he realized he no longer owned a set, he was so furious that, for ten minutes, he'd gone barging around the barracks, slapping the walls, grinding his teeth, and generally muttering under his breath.

Cooling down, he'd switched on the radio and listened without much interest to a phone-in program. At that hour of the morning, though, people wanted to talk about the strangest stuff. There were callers with opinions and statements about things ranging from the politics of gene splicing to the best novelty song ever recorded. Gosh finally dozed off just before dawn and dreamed that he had to fight the Honky Tonk Man in a jungle while constrictor snakes slithered overhead and monkeys laughed.

He woke at eleven, showered, dressed, and gobbled down an NRG stick. Then he got out an old sketchpad, and, flipping through it, found a pencil drawing that he thought looked pretty decent, and redid it on good paper, working quickly.

Gosh was a capable draughtsman—when he drew a dinosaur, by God, it looked like a dinosaur—but he harbored serious doubts about whether his temperament was genuinely "artistic." Although he liked to draw, every time he sat down at his table, he felt tremendous anxiety.

Del Forno said it was career anxiety.

Del Forno, for once, was probably telling the truth.

Career anxiety. Right, right. But that was merely another facet, a subsidiary pang, to Gosh's central anxiety, which was this: He'd been using plastic to pay for everything, from rent to breath mints, since leaving the orphanage two years ago.

According to his last statement from the Central Bank of Beings, headquartered in Boulder, Colorado, he was three million dollars in debt. Three million and change.

Each month he simply remitted the minimum payment due, $478.60, which he always had to borrow from Del Forno. He'd take Del's cash to the post office, then produce his Only-U credit card to buy a money order and a stamp.

This couldn't go on.

He had to start making some money.

His line of credit was five million dollars, same as everybody else's.

And once he's used that up and was classified a Hopeless Debtor?

Gosh preferred not to think about it.

He'd think about Vicki Zomba, instead.

On second thought, he'd simply think about this hypsilophodon which he'd just finished rendering—should he apply a wash to its underbelly, or use Zip-a-tone? He decided on the Zip, and was cutting some out with an X-acto knife when there was a timid knock at the front door.

It was Julie Jeeters. "Am I bothering you? I'm bothering you, aren't I?" she said. "I'm sorry." She took a step backward and nearly toppled off the low stoop. Gosh grabbed her elbow just in time.

She was wearing a pale blue T-shirt, beige slacks, and white sneakers, exactly what Gosh had been wearing last Sunday night when they'd met.

Gosh wondered if she'd dressed this way on purpose or

just by chance. Then he wondered how come he'd even noticed. Ordinarily, he was not the most observant of young men.

"You're not bothering me at all," he said. "It's nice to see you." He threw the door completely open. "Come on in."

The Jeeters's Chevy was parked in front of the barracks, one tire up on the curb.

Julie Jeeters looked at the X-acto knife in Gosh's hand, then, with a bleak, embarrassed smile, said, "I have your TV in the car. Ira didn't find anything useful when he poked around, so, um, he wants to try and get his money back." 41

Gosh said nothing. He just cocked an eyebrow.

"It still works and all," she added. "Honest. I made him show me. I wouldn't've brought it back if he'd messed it up."

"How come he didn't bring it himself?"

"Well—he's kind of busy."

Gosh smiled.

"I'm just his flunky, aren't I? It's really awful. I'm such a wimp." She made her hands into fists and shook them at the sides of her head.

Gosh walked outside and down to the Chevy with Julie Jeeters following. His television was on the back seat, along with several diskette magazines and a few thin bricks of industrial ceramic.

"It still works fine," said Julie. "Honest."

"Did you really win the lottery?"

Her eyelids snapped open. Then she laughed, bright color rising in her face. "Not me—our dad."

Happy to have his TV back, and even happier to have company, Gosh lugged the set into the barracks, the extension cord dragging behind, then set it down on the table. He plugged it in, hooked up the cable, and switched it on, but it was too late—*Baron Mencken's Wonderland* was over. It was noon already. ". . . —een thousand die in Itaperuna earthquake. And we'll have Sal with the latest sports, Carol with the metro weather."

Gosh jabbed the off tablet.

Sheepishly, Julie produced her brother's Only-U card from her straw bag, and Gosh, excusing himself, went to get his credit-card press, which he kept in an antique safe mounted under the wet bar. He also kept his Social Security card in there, his Good Health certificate, his high school diploma tied with a blue ribbon, and several photographs of Vicki Zomba as Lady Sunny-Weather.

He wrote up a credit slip and ran it through the press.

She accepted the receipt, declined the carbons, and said, "Well."

"How's the Jiffy coming along?"

"Oh, I don't pay much attention, unless something goes wrong and Ira needs me." Julie was over at the drawing board, looking down. "Is this a gecko?" she asked.

"It's a dinosaur."

She flushed.

Gosh said, "I should've put something in there for scale. Like a volcano, or something." But in the past whenever he'd drawn volcanos, people had mistaken them for smokestacks. "You feel like going to the park?" he suddenly asked.

It was just that he felt like getting a little air, that's all. It wasn't as if he were *interested* in this Julie Jeeters, or anything. He just, you know, felt like getting some fresh air.

CHAPTER

"Ira had this great scholarship," Julie was saying. "It was a terrific scholarship. It was all expenses paid."

They'd driven to the city park in her car, left it in the free lot by the oxygen reservoir, and were strolling along the embankment. Sunlight dappled the dark green waters of Wonder Bay.

"But he's always been kind of nutty," she said, leaning against the wall. Down below, big rocks were scummy and green. "The High School of Nothing But Science. In North Carolina. Federally funded."

Gosh said, "No fooling." He leaned over the rail and watched a milk carton slosh back and forth in sudsy effluence.

"Big brains there."

"I'll bet."

"But then he had to go and program that stupid demon. Or whatever it was. He's brilliant, but a little irresponsible. I'm responsible as anything, but not too brilliant."

Gosh turned away from the rail and looked directly at Julie. He saw his own face, twice, reflected in the silver lenses of her sunglasses. Sometimes his own good looks embarrassed him. If good looks had been *the* look at the time, he probably could've been a model, or made action movies. But fashion photographers and Hollywood directors were still in love with the "mutant look," and if you weren't physically bizarre, well, they simply weren't interested. Gosh said, "So what happened after Ira got kicked out of school?"

"He came back home. And never got a diploma. It sure was

a lucky thing for him that Daddy won that lottery. If he hadn't, Ira'd be delivering mail, too. The old-fashioned way."

There were two white refreshment trucks parked up ahead, one selling ice cream, the other hot dogs. Julie said she'd like an ice cream, sure, and selected a fudge face on a stick with a pink ball of bubblegum as its nose. Gosh got a plain vanilla cone with sprinkles. He used his credit card.

Then, since they were headed that way anyhow, they cut across the running track and followed the signs to the zoo.

4 4

"So what're you doing with all your money?" Gosh asked, chewing on sprinkles.

"Me? I'm not doing anything. *I* didn't win it. I'm just going to school, like always. Last year I went to driving school. I can drive anything that moves. I could drive a train, I could drive a spaceship. This year I'm going to fashion school. Which is kind of a joke, since I'm pretty lousy at designing stuff. But I can sew. I'm a sewing whiz."

"I'll bet."

Julie looked at him. "Why do you say that?"

"I don't know."

She frowned, then bit the gumball nose off the ice cream head.

At the zoo, the first thing they came to were the cats. A lion fitfully paced its cage, back and forth, back and forth.

"I don't think I'm going to get through fashion school," Julie said. "And even if I do, I probably won't do anything with my degree. I'll probably just waste my entire life." She laughed, and glanced at Gosh. "I'm only kidding."

"Yeah?"

"Yeah," she said. "But not really."

They went into the aviary, where the squawk was deafening and the plumage brilliant. Shadows flashed against glazed brick. Julie read every description card: ringed teal, blue-crowned motmot, scarlet ibis.

They strolled back outside into the white daylight, and, blinking, looked around for where to go next. They headed for the reptile house, a long cinder-block building at the southern end of the zoo. On the way there, Julie stopped to watch a few gophers darting in and out of sandy burrows. "Indigenous to Arizona," she said, reading the card.

Gosh shrugged.

"That's where my father lives now," she said. "Arizona. He bought himself a big ranch. A hacienda, he calls it. Well, he can afford it."

"Sure."

"That's what he always wanted to do, live in the desert. Nice for him."

Gosh smiled.

"He's doing exactly what he wants."

"That's what it means to be rich."

"Oh, yeah," Julie agreed, and moved away from the railing. "I wish I knew what *I* wanted to do."

"You and me both."

Julie seemed happy to hear that.

They continued up the path. Two young girls ran by, clutching silver helium balloons bearing giraffe silouettes. Their mother limped behind, lugging a picnic hamper.

"That hacienda of his," said Julie, "is his only extravagance. Most of the money goes to Ira. Daddy has great faith in Ira. He lets him buy anything he wants, you should see. He even let Ira buy this old factory to work in. We both live there. You should come over some time."

Gosh said nothing, not wanting to commit himself.

She was a nice girl, this Julie Jeeters, but Gosh already *had* a girl. Sort of.

"It's a big old factory that used to make light bulbs."

"Don't you get any of the money?"

"Oh, if I ever need some, all I have to do is ask. But there's nothing I really want."

"Seriously?"

"Well," she said, "I'm sure there must be *something* I want, but I haven't thought of it yet." She smiled, then hooked her arm through Gosh's, but he must've flinched, because only a few seconds later, she withdrew it.

CHAPTER

Gosh inserted his credit card into a lottery machine, punched in a few random numbers, and took his ticket.

The current jackpot, according to the digital readout, was $14 billion.

As they passed out of the zoo shop and started up the ramp toward the dinosaurium, Julie asked, "You come here a lot?"

"Oh, yeah."

She said, "I figured. Seeing that drawing of yours, I figured as much."

They were standing now on the rim of a cement volcano, gazing down into the dinosaur pit, about half the size of a football field.

The prehistoric world had been reproduced adequately enough, with bubbling pools and rocks that looked still new, and with trees and shrubbery and stuff that hadn't existed for several million years. If you looked closely, though, you could see, in several places, some exposed metal and riveting on a cliff, where the paint had been scratched away. Things needed a little sprucing up.

"When I was a kid," Gosh said now, "I used to come once a year."

"Your parents take you?"

"The orphanage. It was a big excursion. Everybody went."

"You were an orphan?"

Gosh smiled. "Still am."

"How'd your parents die?"

He shrugged. "I was one of those guys left on a doorstep."

"You're kidding! That's great! How old were you?"

"Almost two. I think. At least the orphanage decided I was two, and started counting from there."

"What, like you had a note pinned to your shirt or something?"

Laughing, Gosh said, "No. I just showed up with the clothes on my back. And I was carrying a vinyl dinosaur. Triceratops."

4 8

"You don't remember who left you there?"

He shook his head.

"That's wild."

"And the only word I spoke was *gosh*. So they decided to call me Joe Gosh."

"That's the greatest story I ever heard! Wow!"

"Gosh," he said, and Julie laughed. She studied his face, then blinked, and lowered her eyes.

"Do you remember that iguanodon that used to be here?" she asked. "That used to sit over there on that boulder?" She pointed. "It had these lumps on its throat, a whole bunch of lumps? I guess it must've died. I haven't seen it in years. You remember?"

He nodded, thinking about those orphanage excursions, everybody piling onto big yellow buses, the head counts, the ID labels, the lectures. He remembered hearing about Sawyer's Farm upstate, and about a migrant worker named Hector Geraldino who'd found a cave that led straight down to where a mixed herd of dinosaurs, bona fide though stunted, lived in a grotto.

Gosh smiled, remembering those visits, when he'd go scooting around with Del Forno and a guy named Shrike; remembered, one time, being grabbed by a guard just as he had a leg hitched over the railing. Remembered the red-faced guard shouting, "Where do you think you're going, stupid?" Then the guard saying, as he shook Gosh by the shoulders, "See that one? That's a meat eater!"

Every visit, Gosh had bought a few more dinosaur souvenir cards at the zoo shop, and on the ride back to the orphanage, he'd used a fingertip to outline the glossy pictures. An albertosaurus, a cetiosaurus, a dimetrodon. Later, in the dormitory, he'd trace them, using tissue paper, or copy them into one of his class notebooks. Finally, he'd started drawing them from memory, or his imagination. He was good, his dinosaur pictures were terrific. Anytime he tried drawing something besides a giant lizard, though—a person, say, or a hover car or a videophone—the result was clumsy and amateurish. He could draw dinosaurs, period. That was his only talent, as far as he could tell, and, to say the least, it seemed an unlikely basis for a lucrative career. He could manipulate a pencil, but otherwise he was no good with his hands. He'd flunked shop all through high school. So, work in the building trades was out.

49

Standing with Julie now, he strained his eyes, trying to see whether that grumpy T-Rex, no bigger than a common water buffalo, was still among the herd. He saw the stegosaurus and the plesiosaur, but couldn't spot the tyrannosaur.

In recent years, the dinosaur population had been steadily dying off. There'd never been a single one born in captivity. Kind of sad.

Gosh realized suddenly that Julie was staring at him. When he turned from the rail to look at her, she flushed and glanced away. Then she looked at her watch. "I guess we should be going," she said. "I have to run Ira to the bank before three."

"Boy, you're sure at his beck and call, aren't you?"

She made a sour face. "I'm *such* a wimp," she said. "It's terrible. And it's all my fault, really. When we were kids? We were playing one day—blindman's bluff? So I tied the blindfold on Ira, and while he was walking around, I sneaked up and stood in front of him, and then, with all my might, I hit him in the stomach. That night he went to the hospital and had to have his appendix taken out. I've been sorry ever since."

"That's kind of crazy."

"I know it. I bet you that me hitting him in the stomach and him having his appendix out weren't even related."

"I bet, too."

Julie smiled, displaying her white, slightly crooked, teeth. "But I guess it doesn't matter. There's something about my dopey brain that makes me feel guilty to this day."

Gosh took a last glance at the small herd, then they walked back down the ramp together.

In the zoo shop, Gosh was purchasing a couple of rubber mastodons and a plastic T-Rex tooth on an imitation gold chain, when somebody let out a horrible shriek.

He turned, just in time to see Nippy the dog, and the real estate section from last Sunday's newspaper, materialize over the lottery machine.

CHAPTER

"You saw it, didn't you? Come on, already—I'm not making this up! I could've been killed!" On the man's head was an alpine cap stenciled with a mountain goat and the zoo logo. "There was a dog, I'm telling you!" He gestured wildly.

Gosh shrugged and spread his hands.

The souvenir shop lady rolled her eyes. She'd heard a lot of nutty things in her time, but this took the cake.

Almost as soon as Nippy had appeared, she'd darted through the open doorway in a tan blur. She was here, then gone, in three seconds flat.

Julie had raced after her.

Now, the man in the alpine cap started kicking the lottery machine, demanding a refund. The souvenir lady picked up a telephone and dialed zoo security. Gosh beat it.

Julie had already left the zoo and was scrambling up one of the low hills around the reservoir. Shouting her name, Gosh ran after her, and nearly trampled a peacock by the front gate who'd just fanned open its flashy plumage.

Topping the hill and glancing every which way, he spotted Julie, now down by the serpentine. Nippy was racing in mad circles around her legs. Gosh struck off toward them at a jog.

He hadn't intended to treat this as a big joke, but when he noticed Julie's pallor and the way that she was gulping, he decided that maybe, just maybe, some humor was called for, and said, "Any postage due?"

The wisecrack, however, went over like a lead balloon.

She said, "I'm going to knock his brains in!" Nippy lay down on the grass and whimpered. "Can you believe this? Can you believe he'd put my dog in that stupid machine of his!"

Though he certainly did believe Ira Jeeters capable of such a thing, Gosh said nothing. He just stood there with his hands in his back pockets, staring at Nippy. Her flanks heaved. Her coat was dusted with blue grit. "She looks okay," he finally said, wondering if she might be fireproof.

"I'll strangle him!"

"I doubt that."

Julie made a sound of disgust, possibly of self-disgust, but managed a little smile.

Then, from directly in back of them, came a ringing shout: "That's the dog!"

It was the man in the alpine hat again, being escorted through the front gate by zoo guards.

Gosh said, "I think we should get the heck out of here," and led the way across the great lawn, toward the parking lot.

Nippy kept shaking her head and stopping to gnaw at her upper thigh, but she was apparently over the jimjams and followed Julie docilely.

As they were passing the two refreshment trucks, the dog became frisky again, however, leaping at Julie and barking. "I bet Ira forgot to feed her at noon," she said, frowning. "I bet she's starving, poor thing." She looked at the dog and said, "Sit . . . sit," and Nippy sat. Then Julie ambled over to one of the trucks and joined the end of a short line, to buy a frankfurter.

Gosh stooped and combed his fingers through the animal's coat. He tried to pluck a hair out, but couldn't. And the dog didn't so much as flinch when he tried. His nails came back rimmed with blue sand.

Over at the truck, Julie was placing her order.

A rangy-looking guy in blue jeans and a workshirt, who'd been loitering nearby, tossed away his fudge pop and started walking casually, too casually, toward her. The moment she turned away from the service window with a frankfurter—just the frank, no bun—on a paper plate, he passed behind her and

snatched her shoulder bag, yanking so hard that she lost her balance. The frankfurter sailed skyward.

With Julie's bag clutched to his chest, the guy sprinted away like a halfback—directly toward Gosh, whose head, suddenly, started ringing. Gosh might've tackled the thief without his having realized he'd even been spotted, *if* Gosh hadn't done a stupid thing—if he hadn't shouted, "Stop!"

The thief veered, of course, and went highballing off in another direction.

5 4

Gosh swore at himself and gave chase. But in practically no time at all, he was winded; he'd never been too keen on regular exercise. He stopped, chuffing madly, humiliated.

A moment later, Nippy flew, actually flew, past, riotously barking, and followed the purse snatcher over the top of a knoll.

CHAPTER

The thief was sprawled out, facedown, on the new-mown grass of a softball field. Nippy stood panting on his back. DOG TACKLES THUG. Julie's bag lay several feet away, its contents scattered. A lipstick, an address book, a suede wallet, and several manufacturers' coupons—for spicy mustard, all-beef franks, makeup-remover cloths, and caramel cookie bars. Gosh thought, Her father wins nineteen billion bucks and she clips coupons?

When Nippy heard him coming, her head shot up and she barked again.

By the time Julie trotted down the hill, the amazing dog was gamboling after a breeze-snatched coupon good for five dollars off the purchase of dry-roasted nuts, and Gosh was squatted beside the thief, checking for a pulse. "You got him!" Julie marveled. "Oh, you're terrific!"

Gosh said, "It wasn't—" but stopped, dumbstruck by the dazzling smile on her face. She was positively beaming at him. Swallowing hard and allowing himself the tiniest smile, Gosh said, "It was no big thing."

He felt guilty for taking credit, but what the heck. If she hadn't seen Nippy go flying, what the heck.

He'd never been a hero before, not ever.

It was kind of neat. And so easy, too!

A moment later, however, the big hero cringed when the thief let out a deep groan and rolled sluggishly onto his back.

Immediately, and only because Julie was watching, Gosh straddled the guy's torso, leaned forward, and pinned his arms back. Secretly, he was scared to death, appalled at himself. He recognized the guy—remembered seeing him at Ma's garage the other night, sorting jewelry.

The thief gurgled, spat out a lateral incisor, and opened his eyes. Not blinking, his breathing shallow, he stared at Gosh. Then he asked, seriously, "How come it's light out? What time is it?"

Gosh scowled.

"What *day* is it?"

Julie Jeeters, who'd been gathering up her things and sticking them all back into her bag, laughed. "Bro-*ther*," she said with disdain. "Can you believe that? What's he going to say next, that he's got amnesia? What do you *take* us for, you crook?" she added, coming over and glaring down. But as soon as the zombie turned his head toward her, Julie's bravado died. "Should we call a cop, Joe?"

"You see one?"

Julie looked up and down the ball field, and guessed not.

Then Gosh took a chance and stood up, very slowly. The zombie remained where he was, wiping blood from his split lip and looking altogether perplexed.

"What's going on?" he asked. "What am I doing here? How come my back hurts? I lost a tooth!"

Positioning herself behind Gosh, Julie Jeeters lashed into him once more. "You're a lousy actor," she said. "You're about the lousiest actor I ever saw! You just stole my bag—as if you didn't remember! Don't try to fool us, don't think you can worm your way out of this! Boy, you must think we're the biggest jerks in town."

The zombie sat bolt upright, blinking. "I never snatched a handbag in my life!" He seemed highly insulted. "Not in my life! What do you think I am?"

And Gosh blurted, "A car thief."

Flabbergasted, Julie Jeeters said, "A *what*?" but the zombie just narrowed his foggy eyes, struggling to remember . . . something.

A Caddy Caudillo, perhaps.

Meanwhile, Nippy had plopped down by third base and was scratching the back of her head maniacally, broadcasting blue grit all over the place.

Del Forno said, "I didn't think you'd mind," when Joe Gosh walked into the barracks-house later that afternoon and found his friend stretched out on the sofa practicing a new story.

"I don't," Gosh said, going to the fridge and pulling out a quart of grape juice. He took a swig, wiped his mouth on his forearm, and stuck the can back on a shelf.

Del had a pad of yellow foolscap balanced on his thighs. The top sheet was covered with an illegible scrawl. No-Deposit stood by, a few of its red lights blinking. Del leaned over and punched a tablet on the robot's shoulder. The red lights went out and a few green ones came on. Swinging his legs over the side of the sofa, Del stood up, stretching. "I'm making a story out of that time we got arrested in Maryland. What do you think, you think that'd make a good story?"

"What happened? We got arrested for speeding, we paid a fine. Where's the story?"

Del laughed. "I bet you don't even remember that guy we met in the cell—who used to be a government assassin."

"We were never *in* a cell."

"See? I told you you wouldn't remember." Del laughed again, and jabbed another tablet in No-Deposit's neck. There was the faintest whir of an audio tape rewinding. "You want to hear what I got so far?"

"Del? I have to tell you something."

Del's stage voice, deeper than his normal speaking voice, boomed from the robot's mouth grid. "I have this pal who's the world's worst driver," it said. "You take your life in your hands when you get in a car with him. But I don't like to hurt his feelings, so whenever he calls me up—" Del lowered the volume a tad.

"Who's the pal?" said Gosh petulantly.

"You, of course," said Del with a twitch of a smile.

"—agree to go," said Del's voice.

"What're you *talking* about," said Gosh, "I'm a *good* driver."

"Sssh," said Del.

"Would you please turn that off? Really. I have something to tell you."

Del cocked his head, and obliged.

"Why do you always change things around in your dopey stories?"

"Because," said Del, "in real life, nothing exciting ever happens to me. *That's* why. I couldn't make ten cents telling true stories." He shrugged. "So what's this something you just have to tell me?"

Gosh smiled.

And ten minutes later, Del said, "The dog *flew*?"

"Flew."

"Come on, Joey!"

"Straight over my head."

Del offered a grunt. "See? That's exactly what I mean! About nothing exciting ever happening to *me*! So what'd you do with the zombie?"

"Nothing. We just left him in the park. You should've seen him, Del—totally confused. Last thing he remembers was breaking into a car around midnight, February twentieth."

"And your girlfriend didn't see her dog go zooming?"

"She's not my girlfriend," said Gosh. Then he slowly shook his head. "No, she didn't see."

"And you didn't tell her." Del's eyes glimmered puckishly. "How come?"

Gosh shrugged.

Del thought that was a hoot. "Where are they now, the young lady and her flying dog?"

"On their way home, I guess. They dropped me off." Gosh had gone over to the front window. Across the street, outside the Big Boy restaurant, several teenaged kids with strips of cellophane woven through their green-dyed hair were scarfing burgers and fries. A flatbed truck piled with junk pipe rolled by. "You know that story you swiped from me?" Gosh said at last.

"Which one?"

"About X. S. Powers."

"What about it?"

Gosh watched the mailman steer a letter cart around the corner from Medley Place into Morning Street.

"You don't see the similarity? Come on, Del! I think Ira's Jiffy is punching things into the same—the same *whatever* that Powers passed through in his jet plane. Like, the same *dimension*. I think that's what's going on here."

"Yeah?"

Gosh turned from the window and looked at his friend. "Yeah. And I'm thinking that maybe—" He stopped when today's mail dropped with a whoosh through a brass slot in the front door.

"You're thinking maybe what?" said Del.

Gosh snatched up several bills, a questionnaire from the Census Bureau, a sample bar of a new deodorant soap, and yet another multivolume book offer from Time-Life, Inc. The burst on the envelope said "Accept Volume One—Great Air Battles of the Mosquito War—as OUR FREE GIFT!" Gosh tore it in half and dumped it in a wastebasket. Then he similarly disposed of the rest of his mail.

Impatient, Del said, "You're thinking that maybe *what?*"

And Gosh said, "That Ira's machine is the answer to all my career problems."

CHAPTER

They took Del's Chrysler, which had nearly eighty-one thousand miles on the odometer, dozens of empty aseptic juice cartons on the floorwell, and a TV mounted under the dash. Del gunned the car through orange lights, spurted through every other red one. He was, in Gosh's opinion, the world's worst driver, never signaling, passing on the right, changing lanes on a whim, and glancing at the television screen every three or four seconds.

Gosh wished he still had his own car. But he'd loaned it last year to his good friend Shrike, who'd driven it down to Mexico City and never come back.

He could always just buy a new one, of course, on credit, but so far he'd resisted that temptation. The cheapest Korean imports started at $999,900.

When Del veered onto the sidewalk to pass an oil truck that was being sluggish about making a left turn, Gosh said, "Are you crazy? What's the hurry?"

"Don't you want to solve all your problems?" Del was hunched over the wheel, grinning.

"If I'm dead, I can't solve diddly."

"Where's Avenue M?"

"Right after Avenue L."

They'd just passed the corner of Avenue E.

Del looked at the TV screen, then flicked his eyes back toward the street, and ran another stoplight.

Gosh reached to switch off the set.

"Don't," said Del. "I'm waiting for my tax refund to appear."

"Very funny."

The evening news was on, though Gosh wasn't paying it much attention. Since getting into the car, there'd been some footage of flood debris, a brief story concerning mutant cattle in Utah that glowed in the dark, and all the baseball scores.

They were passing the Guatemalan consulate on Avenue H when a human interest feature about the National Scions Foundation came on. The media loved the scions and their philanthropic exploits, but Gosh had grown weary of all the coverage. Twenty-five filthy rich little boys, big deal. What silly project had they funded today at their latest news conference? Another arbitrage workshop for third-graders?

Grudgingly, Gosh stared at the screen, at five preadolescent males in hundred-thousand-dollar business suits seated nose-high to a boardroom table. Behind them, the foundation's seal—high-top sneakers dangling from a dollar sign—was mounted on the wall.

Gosh's jaw dropped when he heard the spokesboy announce that the organization had just committed thirty million dollars to an Amazon expedition going in search of the Honky Tonk Man.

Del said, "The Honky Tonk Man? Jeeps, they're too young to even *remember* the Honky Tonk Man!" He gave the horn a solid punch, scaring the dickens out of several pedestrians in the crosswalk.

Gosh said, "She got to them."

"Who did?"

"Ma Zomba. Look at their eyes! She got to them. This is her idea."

Del chuckled. "What a waste of money. They're not going to find him. I mean, I bet he's dead."

With a ballpoint pen, the spokesboy was pointing to a map of Brazil, indicating a jungle zone that was dark green.

Gosh looked away from the TV and said, "Del, you passed it!"

Already they were at Avenue O.

Doing sixty, Del made an illegal U-turn, cutting off a panel truck.

Making the left into Avenue M, the tires squealed.

No-Deposit fell over on the back seat.

Gosh said, "Drive a little crazier, why don't you?"

"Don't be sarcastic."

Avenue M was zoned for light manufacturing, but whatever industries once thrived there had failed years ago. Brick building after brick building bore the signs of various Wonder City realtors: Matetsky and Murrah, Bigg and Son, Best-Turf, Inc. Buy. Rent. Available. The ailanthus trees bordering the sidewalks were mostly dead, and those yet alive had had their branches vandalized, their bark stripped. The pavements were strewn with litter. Abandoned cars had been cannibalized— hoods up, guts out, wheels gone.

"Tell me when to stop," said Del.

"Now."

Number Eighty-three Avenue M was a crumbling factory like all the other factories up and down the block. Dimly, Gosh made out a hand-lettered sign bolted to the steel door: Light-of-the-World Bulbs, Inc. The windows were boarded, and the grounds enclosed by a high fence of chain link, its top swirled with razor wire. The gate was padlocked.

Del and Gosh sat in the parked car for half a minute, just looking.

Finally Del said, "If he lets you do it and you don't blow up or vanish or anything, just don't forget who your best friend is, when you're famous."

Gosh smiled. But he was thinking that maybe this wasn't such a great idea, after all.

CHAPTER

Ira Jeeters's laboratory was rigged with so much electronics equipment it made the Pentagon's War Room look like somebody's country kitchen. There were serious computers as big as steam cabinets, consoles bristling with levers, and monitor screens that displayed a dizzying multitude of digits or characters. The air vibrated. At opposite ends of the room stood identical metal stalls which resembled outdoor showers, even down to the cloudy plastic curtains.

Gosh said, "Hey, Ira," like they were buddies.

Jeeters, who'd been highlighting printout equations with a read-through green marker, yelped and whipped around, eyes bugged in surprise. "How the heck did *you* get in here?"

Gosh said, "This is quite a place," feeling it wiser not to answer Jeeters's question.

No-Deposit had simply used a pointing finger to slice off the padlock on the fence, a pinky to force open the front door. From there, it had been easy to find the laboratory, only a matter of following resonant hums up a flight of iron steps to their source on the second floor.

Jeeters, charming as always, said, "If you got some complaint about your TV, stuff it." He was wearing a lab coat, riveted dungarees, and deck shoes.

"No complaints, none," said Gosh, and his overly friendly tone of voice aroused Jeeters's suspicions. He closed one eye and quirked his mouth.

"What do you want?"

"Ira? This is my good pal, Del Forno. And that's No-Deposit."

Ira glanced briefly at the robot, then said with contempt, "How come you waste your money on one of those cheap things? It's got beans for memory."

Del took offense. "But a lot of heart. That counts."

"If you're looking for my sister," said Jeeters, "she's not here. And I don't know when she'll be back. So you-all can just leave now."

Gosh nodded, but ambled over to one of the shower-stall contraptions. He pulled back the curtain. It was deceptively heavy, like a dental X-ray bib, only sized for a giant.

"Don't touch," said Ira.

"This it? This the Jiffy?"

"Is *that* it?" said Del. "Jeeps, I don't know if I'd want to have a thing like *that* in my apartment." He looked at Jeeters "I never get all that much mail, anyhow."

Jeeters's back stiffened. "Did you tell this person about my project?" he said, shaking a finger stiffly at Gosh. "You had no right! I *knew* I should've made you sign an agreement of confidentiality! I told Julie that."

"Where *is* Julie?"

"Out."

"You guys have a big argument?"

Jeeters opted not to answer.

Gosh tapped the side of the Jiffy. "What do you do, you just put the stuff in here? Letters, parcels, magazines . . . dogs."

Jeeters's face darkened. "I did *not* put that animal in there on purpose! I had to listen to Julie, now I have to listen to you? I was preparing to send a stack of old newspapers and the silly dog sat down on top of them. I couldn't get her out."

"So you just sent her, too?" Gosh smiled.

"I'm on a very tight schedule."

Gosh said, "This is the transmitter, and"—nodding toward the identical Jiffy standing flush against the opposite wall—"that's the receiver? Or is this the receiver?"

"You had it right the first time. Now will you please go?"

Instead, Gosh sat down at a console. On the screen were cybernetic symbols in three-dimensional configurations he'd never seen on any high school terminal. "You get a chance to examine Nippy?" he said.

Jeeters pressed his lips together, clearly chagrined. "Hardly. I'm lucky that fleabag didn't chew my leg off."

"Mad at you, huh?" said Del. He and No-Deposit had ensconced themselves on an unpadded banquette.

Gosh leaned against the Jiffy with his arms folded, like Mr. Cool, and said, "I have a proposition to make, Ira. All in the name of science."

CHAPTER

"Oh, sure," said Jeeters, "and what happens if you reassemble with your eyes in the back of your head—you won't sue? Don't kid me, Gosh. Don't take me for an idiot."

"You want me to sign something first, I'll sign."

"Forget it. The Jiffy is strictly for mail."

One of the consoles in the lab had turned out to be a disguised refrigerator. While Gosh had pitched his scheme, offering himself as parcel post, Jeeters had opened the freezer door and taken out a quart of vanilla-fudge ice cream. He used a plastic spoon, eating directly from the carton, and never offering Gosh or Del so much as a taste. Digging out yet another spoonful now he said, "Why?"

"Why?"

"Would you make this crazy offer. Yeah: why?"

Gosh shrugged. "I'm a thrill-seeker."

Over in the corner, Del laughed.

"And I'll be famous," Gosh quickly added.

It was Jeeters's turn to laugh. "Name the first man on Mars."

Gosh thought, but couldn't remember.

"See?"

This exchange was too good for Del to let slip by: he jabbed the Record button in No-Deposit's neck.

Jeeters, enjoying himself now, said to Gosh, "Keep going. More whys."

"I'll get rich."

"Stop!" Jeeters pressed the round lid on the ice-cream carton and stuck it back in the freezer. "How do you figure on getting rich? It's my invention."

"Personal appearances."

"You're out of your mind. Who'd pay good money to see some schnook who had his molecules scrambled?

"Nobody," said Gosh. Then, fed up, he said, "For a guy who's supposed to be such a big brain, you're sure dense, Ira. The scissors broke! The mail wouldn't burn."

"Glory be! Are you a piece of paper?"

"Is Julie's dog?"

"You tried to burn *Nippy?*" Jeeters started to make a derisive face, but quit before his lips had fully crimped. Then he cocked an eyebrow. "What are you saying?"

So, at last, Gosh told him about the incident in the park.

"Julie said *you* caught that guy."

"She assumed I did." Gosh reddened. "But I didn't."

Frowning, and tapping his lips with two fingers, Jeeters paced the lab. Gosh stood, arms akimbo, watching him.

At last, Jeeters stopped. "The receiver still doesn't work. You could end up anywhere."

"I thought about that. But listen, Ira. My house, the zoo, St. John's church, even—they're all within a couple of miles of here. So it's not very likely that I'd . . . come out on the moon, or someplace."

Ira nodded, pacing again.

Again he stopped. "It's entirely possible you could reassemble in an occupied space, instead of above it. Know what would happen then?"

Gosh didn't, and felt that he'd rather not, but Ira told him anyway.

Actually, Ira didn't tell him, but merely created an explanatory sound effect. He said, *"Ka-blam!"*

Gosh managed a thin smile.

"You'd take that risk?"

"Sure." He wished he felt as cocky as he sounded.

Propelling himself across the floor, like a prosecuting

attorney going for blood, Jeeters exclaimed, "Sure! Sure, why not? If my Jiffy does a job on you, out you come a fricken superman! The idol of Wonder City."

"Maybe even the world," Del chipped in.

"Well, who does anything risky for *nothing*?" said Gosh.

"Exactly," said Jeeters. "So why should I let you take a free ride?"

Gosh exhaled noisily.

"So why should I—huh?"

Del said, "No free rides. Now, where'd I hear that before?"

Gosh said, "How much, Ira?"

"Well . . . how much credit do you have left with the Bank of Beings?"

Gosh felt his stomach fold in half, then fold in half again.

"Come on, how much?"

Del sprang to his feet. "Joey? Let's get out of here. The whole idea was crazy to start with."

Gosh was staring dully at the amazing shower stall.

"Deal," he finally said.

CHAPTER 17

Jeeters insisted on taking care of all the dreary paperwork before he'd allow Gosh to set even one foot inside the Jiffy.

First, Gosh had to sign an agreement never to litigate. No matter what happened. Reluctantly, Del witnessed it.

Then Jeeters telephoned Boulder, Colorado, and, after reading all thirty-eight digits, plus the expiration date, on Gosh's Only-U card, ascertained how much credit remained available. Three million, one hundred nine thousand, six hundred forty-two dollars, and seventeen cents.

The simple contract was then drawn up, using that figure, down to the last penny.

By that time, Gosh was seeing red and black spots whizzing back and forth in front of his eyes. He had to sit down and breathe deeply.

"I'm not in the science racket for my health, you know," said Jeeters. "There's nothing wrong with obscene profits."

When he and Gosh had both signed the contract, Gosh handed it to Del for his signature. But Del balked.

"No way, José."

"You're not liable," said Jeeters. "We just need a witness."

"Well, find somebody else. I refuse to be a part of this."

"Please," said Gosh. "Everything's going to be cool."

Del folded his arms stubbornly.

Turning to Jeeters, who hadn't stopped grinning since the terms were set, Gosh asked, "Could you leave us alone for a couple of minutes?"

"Sure. But only a couple. I might change my mind." Jeeters stepped outside to wait on the factory landing.

"He's whistling," said Del.

"He's a real creep, what can I tell you?"

"That you're not really going to do this thing."

"I thought you were all for it."

"Yeah, sure, when I figured it was only a question of life and death. When either you'd never come out, or you'd come out the new X. S. Powers. But now it's serious. Now there's big money involved."

"It'll work."

"But what if it doesn't? What if you come out the same way you went in? Still a nobody, your credit all used up."

Doggedly, Gosh said, "It'll work. I'll be a celebrity. I'll make tons of money. Vicki Zomba will think I'm the greatest. So will her mother. I won't have a single problem left in the world. It'll *work*, Del. I'll make tons of money. Vicki—"

"If it doesn't work, you'll spend the rest of your life sweat-equitying your debt away. You want to live in a quonset hut? You want to be a *miner*? You want to live on *Mars*?"

"Vicki Zomba will think I'm the greatest," said Gosh. "So will her mother."

Del threw up his hands. He looked over at No-Deposit, then shrugged and muttered, "Well, I tried."

Gosh said, "Should I tell Jeeters to come back in now?"

Del moistened his lips and nodded.

CHAPTER

Standing hunched inside the Jiffy like a subway commuter, Gosh was impatient to be off before his fading courage faded completely. He looked as though he needed a blood transfusion, he'd gone that pale. His heart faltered, his breath was raspy, and his head teemed with fugitive memories: of an excursion to the dinosaurium when he was sixteen and still woozy, half-delirious, from a recent bout of flu . . . of the day he'd bought a hamburger at the Big Boy restaurant and discovered a sliver of glass between lettuce and pickle . . . of the time that he and Shrike had tossed a cherry bomb into a urinal, not realizing that the fuse was waterproof. They'd intended only to scare Del, who was such a cringer. They'd never meant for the bomb to actually blow . . . but it had, it sure enough had, and ruptured the entire plumbing system in the orphanage. Crazy things to be thinking about at a time like *this*.

Ira was bent over a control panel, gleefully flipping toggles and fine-tuning various doodads.

Across the lab, Del chewed on his fingernails. No-Deposit sat next to him on the banquette, its chest lights twinkling and surging like the bands on a preamp.

"Get ready to hold on," said Ira.

Gosh asked, "To what?"

"Well . . . just kind of brace yourself, then."

Gosh swallowed, glanced at Del, and managed a gallows smile.

"When you get where you're going," said Del, "make sure

you call us, I'll come pick you up. You have some change on you?"

Gosh didn't, but figured he could simply charge the telephone call. But wait! he thought. I can't. I'm broke. A Hopeless Debtor!

At that realization, he panicked and very nearly leapt free of the Jiffy.

Suddenly, however, loud buzzing noises started in his head, and dots of colored light squirmed through his field of vision.

Del's face seemed to elongate, then to smear.

This'll be great, Gosh thought.

It'll work.

He was petrified.

And then, in the last few moments prior to his passing out of sight, all this occurred:

Nippy the dog came blasting through the lab wall, sending chunks of lathing and Sheetrock in every direction.

Then Julie appeared, entering by the door with two sacks of groceries in her arms and saying, "Ira? I think there's something wrong with Ni—"

Then she spotted Gosh, but before she had time even to register that particular surprise, Del stepped briskly forward. "You must be Julie. Delbert Forno. I believe Joey told you a little something about me."

Then the spaniel, tail bristling, jaws clashing, commenced barking at Ira Jeeters like a dog of another, heavier, more lethal breed.

And then Gosh—shutting his eyes tight, clenching his teeth, and silently counting one-Mississippi, two-Mississippi— was spirited away.

CHAPTER

He still had the sense of his body: spine prickly, lungs working, cheeks flush. He felt whole, physical; himself. And he kept falling, till with a painful thump, he hit bottom.

Bottom of what?

He was sprawled out on a voluptuous dune of blue sand. Stretching away in every direction was an undulant Sahara of the same stuff: pale blue nearby, and darker blue, almost purple, in the far, crisp distance. The air was cool and moist. Moist, cool air in a desert? Overhead, the sky was turbulent and white, like empty airwaves on a television screen.

Gosh stayed where he'd fallen on his back, afraid to move. His legs ached and his coccyx hurt. Sand sifted down his shirt collar. He thought, I'm going to kill Ira Jeeters.

Then he thought, Yeah? And how am I supposed to do that?

He shut his eyes again and resumed counting: Mississippi forty-three . . .

. . . forty-four.

When, timidly, Gosh uncracked an eye once more, he was still there. Rubbing a hand across a cheek, his skin crackled with grit. After he'd let his arm drop, however, he continued to hear the crackling sound. He sat bolt upright, then noticed, perhaps twenty feet away, a subtle burrowing movement below the sand.

He tried to get up, but the sand kept spraying out from under his sneakers, from under his hands and knees. He kept slipping and sliding, moving slightly higher up the slope of the dune, but getting nowhere, really.

Then his fingers closed on something, and he flinched.

It was a tiny gray triangle, the corner of an envelope, which bore the Sierra Club logo.

Which meant, Gosh realized, that not everything Jeeters had popped into the Jiffy machine had gotten . . . through.

Right then and there he probably would've thrown himself down in a fit of hopelessness, if something blue, and roughly the size and shape of a human heart, hadn't suddenly popped up from the sand, opened its maw and clamped teeth around his left ankle.

But they didn't puncture his flesh. Instead, they broke, like pretzel sticks.

And when Gosh, instinctively, shook his leg, he flung the critter off with startling ease and sent it flying, straight up. It disappeared with a bright flash.

But all around him now, the sand was eddying, and here, there . . . there (and there, too!) more plump blue things began to appear, a sort of clear mucus spuming from their spongy valves.

Gosh stood immobile, breath scratchy, till something snagged his right tube sock. Then he screamed, like the babysitter in a scary movie, and jumped.

Boy, did he ever jump! A good hundred, hundred fifty feet. There was a loud hiss, butter on a hot skillet, and then, just like that, Gosh vanished, into the streaming, chaotic sky.

CHAPTER

At the sound of jabbering voices, he opened his eyes. Immediately, the talking stopped, and half a dozen antic faces stared down at him: five middle-aged women and a man who was bald except for a fringe of wiry gray hair above each ear. Four of the women were dressed in matching blue frocks. The fifth had a diagonally striped bib pinned around her throat. The man wore a summerweight business suit, white shirt, no tie.

Gosh lay on the floor, surrounded by clumps of different-color human hair. An electric styling comb spluttered weakly by his elbow. He sat up, causing everyone to step back, and huddle.

"Don't you move again till the police come," said the boldest of the blue-smocked women. Her name, Helen, was fancy-stitched on the pocket.

Gosh tried to speak, but his tongue was thick and his mouth full of sand. Bracing himself on the arm of a hydraulic chair, he got slowly to his feet, making certain that he kept up a genial, nonthreatening smile. But when he caught sight of himself in the mirror that ran the full length of the room, he gasped. His face was sweat-streaked with blue grime.

The bald man was off in the corner now, using a pay phone. Gosh heard him say, "That's right—poof! Like some kind of genie. Right on top of Blanche, and her with her back problems! One of my girls—Blanche! She turns on a comb? And this guy flattens her. Yeah, he's still here."

"Here" was a hair-cutting parlor. There were bottles of

tonic and scent and canisters of talc standing on a marble counter, and hanging underneath was a battery of blowers, clippers, and dryers. Taped to the walls were color travel posters—the Parthenon, a parrot in a jungle, and an island girl, her jet-black hair full of red blossoms.

Groggily, Gosh moved toward the front door, and with every step he took, sand sprinkled off his clothing. Through the plate window, he could see people strolling on the pavement. It was twilight.

Suddenly, Helen stepped in front of Gosh, blocking his exit. She'd armed herself with a pair of stainless-steel scissors.

"Excuse me," he said, but the sand in his mouth made his voice sound like a cross between a cat's growl and a woodwind instrument.

The bald man cracked down the phone receiver, hard. "Be careful, Helen! He sounds like a foreigner. He could be dangerous!"

Gosh decided to make a dash for it. He almost hoped that the surly beautician would take a stab at his arm as he jostled past, just so he could determine whether or not the Jiffy had done its job. But she was all bluff, and scurried away the moment it was clear that this, this *foreigner* was for sure going out that door.

Gosh started jogging, glancing up at the first street sign that he passed. It said Ditmar Boulevard, and the cross street was Avenue V. Mentally, he ran through the alphabet, backward. V, U, T, S . . .

Avenue M was nine blocks south.

He dashed across the intersection, against the light, and was struck by a pink Cadillac Caudillo.

CHAPTER

21

"They're wondering where your broken body went," said Shrike the cop. He nodded toward the street, at two medics standing slack-jawed on the curb, looking chagrined and baffled. Thirty seconds ago they'd clambered out of an orange-and-white ambulance from Medical Center IV, adrenalined for emergency action.

An Hispanic guy in grungy coveralls stepped through the door of a discount-muffler shop. He strode over to the medics and said something, punctuating it with rapid-fire hand gestures. Then all three gazed up at the big Meineke sign—specifically, at the deep crease driven into it earlier by Joe Gosh's head. "They're wondering," said Shrike, "how anybody could've bounced off that thing and just walked away. Me, too."

Gosh said, "Yeah."

The pink Caddy had been hooked up to the tow cable of a police wrecker. A cop in a baseball-style cap was finagling with the winch controls. Three other blues were trying to get a statement from the Caddy's languid T-shirted driver, but the procedure didn't appear to be going smoothly: one of the officers kept balling up accident-report forms and tossing them away. At last, the cops conferred, then snapped bracelets on the driver—a zombie, you bet—and stuck him in the prowl car.

Gosh turned away from the window and looked steadily across the table at Shrike, at the precinct number, shield, and nameplate pinned on his summer-uniform shirt. Shrike, a motorcycle cop! Well, why not? Already he'd been—let's see, now—a stockbroker, a deputy mayor, a fight manager, and God knows what else.

The thing about Shrike was, people liked him, and trusted him, the very moment they met him, then gave him, gladly, whatever he wanted. Anything at all. If, for example, Shrike decided to work this month as a chef in a French restaurant, he'd simply waltz into the first Chez Such-and-such that he found, inquire about a job, and be hired on the spot, previous experience be damned. It was almost spooky.

84   Del Forno used to wonder if Shrike's parents had agreeably kicked the proverbial bucket after he'd expressed to them an interest in living childhood as an orphan.

Once, when they'd been discussing his ingratiating effect on others, Shrike had said to Gosh, "I think it must be pheromones." Gosh had never heard that word before, and asked Shrike what it meant. "It's, like, a smell. It must be that I smell good. Don't you think?" Gosh had sniffed, but hadn't been able to detect any unusual odors—any magic smell—wafting off his friend and former dormitory mate. "I mean," Shrike had continued, "why else would everybody think I'm so terrific? I'm pretty ordinary."

True enough. He had a quick, tremendously engaging smile, but a plain, round, forgettable face. And as for his talents, brother, were they meager. All his prizefighters had lost, all his recommended stocks plummeted, and presiding at city council meetings, he'd invariably dozed off before even item 3 on the agenda was reached. He flitted from job to job, from place to place, by nature a sampler. A mediocrity, blessed with charisma.

Gosh had not seen Shrike in almost ten months. Not since Shrike had borrowed Gosh's Ford to drive down to Mexico City, to try guerrilla fighting for a while. When he'd left, Shrike still hadn't had his mind made up whether to join the Communists or a right-wing death squad. He'd play it by ear, he said. Just see what happens.

But now here he was again—a Wonder City cop!—having

coffee and layer cake with Gosh in the Mirabel Diner, while outside the wrecker drove off with the impounded Caddy and the medics scratched their heads.

After Gosh had sailed across Ditmar Boulevard and hit that muffler sign on the fly—the Caddy had been doing sixty— he'd dropped to the pavement like an office safe in a slapstick comedy. His clothes were untorn, and his head—his head was perfect! A little groggy, but otherwise undamaged. He'd wandered over to a sheltered bus stop and sat down on the bench. When the first cop arrived, on a Harley-Davidson, it was Officer Shrike, wearing mirrored sunglasses. He'd strode up to Gosh and said, "Boy, and I always thought that *I* was lucky!"

Now, checking his smile (and what a great smile it was!) in the chromium napkin dispenser, he asked, "So what's going on, Joseph? How'd your head get so hard?"

Gosh tipped a packet of artificial sweetener over his coffee cup. "You have to promise me you won't tell anybody. Not a soul."

Shrike nodded, then listened impassively. When Gosh was finished with his story, though, Shrike struck the table in sheer delight.

"So what're you going to do now?"

Gosh had to restrain himself from laughing, he felt so—so exuberant. "Well, it depends on what I *can* do, I guess. I'll have to check things out."

"Run an inventory."

Gosh nodded. "So to speak."

"See if you can fly and stuff."

"Right, right."

"See if you can stick your tongue in an electric socket. Stop bullets with your teeth."

Gosh said, "What?"

The waitress had been approaching the table, to refill their coffee cups. But now, seeing the police officer suddenly draw his service revolver and point it at the guy with blue sand in his blond hair, she stopped dead in her tracks. A little squeaking noise escaped her ruby lips, but the moment Shrike glanced around, gracing her with his irresistible smile, she rolled her eyes and lifted a shoulder in a semicomic pantomime.

—As if to say, Oh, go ahead and shoot him. Go right ahead! If that's what you really want to do, honey.

CHAPTER

"The auto pound? Hey, Julie—we delivered whozzits to the auto pound."

"Ira, shut up." said Gosh. "It was a hair-cutting parlor, if you really want to know. I'm at the auto pound *now.*"

"What're you doing there?"

Gosh sighed, glancing around the tiny, brightly lit gate shack. Tacked up over the desk were several police memos, a few matte snapshots, and a computer-generated sign that said "Please Be Prepared to Show Driver's License and Valid Registration. Cash or Certified Check Only." Through a window, brilliant vapor lamps illuminated scores of impounded vehicles. A high chain-link fence surrounded the parking lot. There was a rank smell from the polluted river nearby.

"Is Del still at your place?"

"Sure is," said Ira. "He's been trying to make time with my sister."

"Could you put him on the phone, please?"

A moment later, Del said, "Joey, what're you doing at the dog pound?"

"The *auto* pound."

Del said, "Oh." Then he said, "Everything okay? Head on your neck? Feet still pointing in the right direction?"

Gosh smiled. "Everything's fine."

"I'll come pick you up. Gimme directions."

"I can get back by myself. You going to stick around there awhile?"

"Sure. You know that Julie? She's really great, isn't she? I think I'm in love. The only thing is, she's worried sick about you."

Gosh was flattered, but didn't want to think about Julie Jeeters. Not now, at least. There was too much other stuff crowding his brain. "I'm with Shrike," he said.

"What?"

"Shrike. I met Shrike. He's a cop now."

"No fooling!" Del laughed.

"But already he's talking about quitting."

"Tell him I said hi. Quitting? Well, that's nothing new."

"To become my booking agent."

Before Del could say another word, Gosh chuckled and hung up the receiver. He was still feeling goofy, giddy, and having a fine old time.

As he turned away from the desk, he noticed one of the snapshots stuck to the wall. It was a picture of a smiley-faced soldier posed with a flamethrower. One booted foot was planted on the crisped body of a mosquito from Mars. Gosh recognized the teenaged soldier as the fortyish policeman chatting outside in the parking lot with Shrike.

"Del said to say hello."

Shrike nodded, and followed Gosh across the macadam, to the Caddy Caudillo. Lightning flickered. Some distance away yet, thunder boomed. Gosh regarded the crumpled front end of the snazzy car, then peeked through a fist-sized hole in the driver's window. All that remained of the hoodoo altar was the paper dessert plate, which was glued to the dash. The bones, pigeon feathers, and juice cans were scattered in the footwell. The transistor radio lay on the passenger's bucket seat.

"How'd you know you were hit by a stolen car?"

Gosh grinned at Shrike across the rumpled hood.

"And how come you wanna wait for the owner to come claim it? What's the deal, Joseph? Who the heck is Mrs. Zomba?"

"You don't know?"

Shrike shook his head.

"Some cop you are."

"Hey, I've been in Mexico!"

"Speaking of that, where's *my* car?"

"Please," said Shrike, flashing his smile—and, quite possibly, exuding his pheromones—"don't mention that again," and Gosh, unaccountably charmed, didn't.

Instead, he stooped next to the Caddy and reached an arm behind a front quarter panel. Using only a fingertip, he popped the dent.

"Pretty neat," said Shrike as Gosh turned over on his back and wriggled underneath the car. "A rewarding career in body work awaits you."

"I got bigger plans." Bracing both palms against the chassis, Gosh shoved. The Caddy wobbled, then rose. Gosh held it up with his elbows locked. No strain, no pain.

He heard Shrike whistle appreciatively.

Then, letting his left hand drop, he held the Caddy with just his right. The car scarcely tipped. A dollop of oil plashed on his forehead, approximately where Shrike had shot him back at the diner. Shrike had aimed for his mouth, but Gosh flinched. The ricocheting bullet had drilled a hole in the stainless coffee urn.

Without a grunt, Gosh lowered the car, gently.

As he was squirming out from under it, he spotted a pair of red ballet slippers.

And once again—how many times did *this* make?—he was lying flat on his back, staring fixedly up at Ma Zomba.

89

CHAPTER

The police officer who'd once been a soldier in the Mosquito War and now worked four-to-midnight at the auto pound came trotting across the parking lot with a clipboard. "You'll have to sign a couple of forms," he told Ma. "And you gotta show me some proof of identity."

Reluctantly, Ma slid her withering gaze from Gosh to the officer. When her eyes met his, he blinked rapidly, as though she'd just blown illegal smoke in his face. "Well," he said, his voice sounding thick, "I guess we can skip the ID. I'm sure you are who you say you are."

Ma smiled, and signed her name three times, scribbling it like a celebrity. Then she rudely smacked the officer in his chest with the clipboard. He said, "Thank you," and gave her the ignition key. With a sheepish glance at Shrike, he turned and drifted back toward his shack.

Joe Gosh had stood up in the meantime, and now was leaning against the side of the Caddy, acting nonchalant. And acting is the word for it, all right. His heart was throwing a tantrum.

"Are you responsible for this?" Ma asked him, then moistened her lips as she blandly surveyed the damage—the broken headlights and blinkers, the ruined grille, the mangled fender.

Keeping his eyes averted from hers, Gosh replied, "In a manner of speaking."

There was a long silence, during which Ma Zomba fiddled with her dangerous necklace, and the zip-dots on her tent dress accelerated and collided, producing bright pink photon charges.

A drizzle began to fall.

"So how's Vicki doing?" Gosh said at last.

That did it. "I believe I've had enough of you," Ma said. "Get in the car. You drive." Her way of telling him: Say toodle-oo to your free will.

Gosh pressed an index finger across his top lip, suppressing a grin. Then he said, "No."

"Look at me, you little waste of time!"

Gosh said, "How about you look at *me*," then wrenched the driver's door off its hinges and folded it in half as though it were a tabloid newspaper. Then he leaned across the roof panel, dug in his fingertips, and ripped. It came away with the windshield attached. He flung it aside. Then he walked around the Caddy—"Excuse me, Shrike; pardon me, Ma"—and kicked a hole in every sidewall. At last, for good measure, he disjoined the hood, reached into the housing, and plucked out the engine. He lobbed that over the fence. It made a loud splash in mid-river.

Tingling with glee, Gosh wiped his hands of grease, oil, glass, and enamel, using his shirt as a rag. "So what do you think of your blue-eyed boy *now,* Mrs. Zomba?"

The Queen of Crime looked down at the Caddy roof lying at her slippered feet, then cocked her head, perplexedly.

"He also does birthday parties," said Shrike. "Graduations, fund-raisers, corporate retreats, you name it. Rates upon request."

CHAPTER

"Well, we've heard of broken hearts and hearts of stone . . ."

"And don't forget plastic hearts!"

"Plastic hearts, you betcha! And transplanted hearts."

"Even heart swaps! Remember last summer, Ken, when President Cooney and Premier Simferopol exchanged hearts to kick off International Cooperation Year?"

"Who could forget! There's always been a lot of heart in the news, Cathy, but this is the first time—correct me if I'm wrong!—that we've ever reported a heart in a horse race!"

The two anchors paused to simper telegenically.

Gosh filled his cheeks and puffed.

He'd put on the late news to see if there was anything on it about a guy who'd suddenly appeared in a beauty parlor.

"The picture's not so good," said Julie. "Do you want me to try to fix it?"

"Yeah," said Jeeters, "whyn't you do that?"

But before Julie could touch the TV, Gosh said, "Just leave it." She snatched her hand back and clenched it.

On the screen appeared videotaped footage of a Thoroughbred race run earlier that evening. As the horses rounded the far turn, the voiceover said, "Now, get ready to look, folks. Keep your eyes peeled."

"Jeeps!" said Del Forno, leaping up from the sofa.

The blue heart—the same one, no doubt, that Gosh had flung off his ankle and into that white-noise sky—materialized above the pulsing tote board. It tumbled through the air and landed on the turf, then scuttled directly under the hooves of Delightful, Delovely, the easy favorite, who trampled it to paste.

"Whoops!" said Ken and Cathy, together, and Julie, pressing her lips together in distaste, switched off the set.

"Poor thing," she said.

Gosh had already told everybody everything.

On foot and in the pouring rain, he'd arrived at the lightbulb factory almost an hour ago. He'd crouched in front of the fence, then leapt over it. Euphoria! After going inside and up to the lab, he'd peeked through the hole in the wall that Nippy had made. Nobody was around, so he'd traipsed up another flight, to a suite of offices that served as the Jeeterses' apartment, and found Ira, Julie, Del, and No-Deposit playing Monopoly. The robot had hotels on Boardwalk and Park Place and a lot of cash in neat piles. All of Del's property cards were facedown on the bridge table, mortgaged. Ira was in jail. Julie had just landed on Chance.

Gosh had exclaimed, "Ta-da!"

Del was saying now, "Just where the heck did Joey go—do you think?"

Jeeters shrugged. "What's it matter?"

"It's just . . . well, blue hearts and all! Aren't you interested?"

"What *interests* me," said Jeeters, "are results. And their commercial application." He jiggled his eyebrows.

And suddenly Gosh felt his spirits plunge.

It was twenty minutes past eleven.

"You look worried, Joey. What's the matter?"

"Nothing." He smiled at Del, then clasped his hands together behind his head and looked toward Ira Jeeters, who was pacing the carpet thoughtfully.

"Good!" said Del. "So let's go celebrate." He'd already invited everybody over to the Blue Robot, his treat. Besides Del, however, the only person at all keen on the party idea was Julie Jeeters. She went off to put on her dancing shoes, and to set out bowls of fresh food and water for Nippy. The dog was sleeping on the kitchenette floor; had been ever since Gosh came in. "Get happy, guy, you're Mr. Terrific! You did it!"

Gosh nodded tiredly, not taking his eyes off Jeeters, whose mobile grin was beginning to make Gosh very anxious.

Commercial application!

Am I the world's thickest dope, thought Gosh, or what?

Del said, "Hey, wait a second. Where's Shrike?"

Gosh glanced momentarily away from Jeeters. "He went back to police headquarters. To turn in his badge."

"He's serious, he wants to be your agent?"

"That's what he says."

"Well, if that's what he says, that's that."

Rubbing a hand across his jaw, then squeezing his neck with it, Gosh muttered, "I guess so."

Jeeters had quit pacing and was standing still now, hugging himself and nibbling at his bottom lip. His eyes looked unnaturally bright and avid. Did he have commerce on his brain? Was he estimating how much loot he could earn— billions? trillions?—by selling joyrides on the Jiffy? Well, too bad, if so. Too bad for Jeeters. Too, too bad, said Gosh to himself. And was much startled at the bluntness of his sudden resolve.

Clearly, all the changes he'd undergone this long summer evening weren't strictly metabolic.

"That's better!" said Del. "That's the ticket!"

Because Gosh was now smiling from ear to ear.

CHAPTER

Motoring through the Retro District, Del Forno got silly, and, using shopfronts for inspiration, began to recite a litany of catchy alter-ego names for Gosh's consideration. "How about," he said, "you call yourself . . . the Crimson Impala?" Impala Stationery Supplies. "Mr. Odeon?" The Odeon Cinema Six.

"What the heck is an odeon?" asked Julie, who was sitting in back, squeezed between her brother and the robot.

"All right," said Del, who couldn't answer the question. "Forget that. What about—what about Mighty Joe Gosh?" Mighty Fast Dry Cleaners. "Mighty Joe Gosh?"

Unamused, Gosh nevertheless forced a laugh.

"Captain Control?" Comfort Control Vinyl Replacement Windows. "Ideal Man?" Ideal Truck Rental. "*Capital* Man?" Capital Drug and Surgical Sales Company.

Jeeters chuckled, then snidely added his two cents. "How about plain Mr. Wow?"

Then: "Hey!" said Del. "What's going on over there?"

They were passing the Hot Block housing project, a conglomeration of twenty-five or thirty dilapidated orange pyramids. A quarter of a million one-room apartments. The cheapest rentals in Wonder City, for hard-luck cases whose credit was dwindling down down down. Once a week, usually on Wednesday, you'd see fifty or sixty insolvents, each lugging a single piece of soft luggage, file leadenly aboard a courtesy bus from Mars Copper & Realty (a Central Bank of Beings company, which, in turn, was a wholly owned subsidiary of US

Congress, Inc.). Next stop, the Space Port. In the recent past, Gosh, because of his own dire credit straits, had gone out of his way to avoid Hot Block. He preferred not to risk catching a glimpse, thank you, of his potential—his very likely—fate as a welsh miner.

But it wasn't a bus that Del saw now on the plaza, it was a mobile stage, where several actors costumed as gondoliers were serenading a lady on a Venetian balcony. A crowd of perhaps a thousand people sat out in the misty drizzle, watching. Above the stage, the names of the mayor and each and every member of the city council twinkled digitally. Brought to you by, brought to you by, brought to you by . . .

Del had slowed down to look, and to snicker, but now some irritable drivers behind him were honking, so he accelerated. Just as he did, though, the leading lady on the balcony began to sing, and Gosh flinched. As distorted as it was by the antiquated sound system, the tremolo voice unquestionably belonged to the one, the only, the adorably untalented Vicki Zomba!

"Stop!" said Gosh

But Del raced another light, hung an illegal left, and said, "I got it! Astral Man!"

Astral Travel Service—Where Your Money Travels Far.

"Enough!" said Gosh.

"Hey, Joey, it's only show biz," said Del, and when Gosh raised his eyebrows a trifle, he added, "We're only kidding around, jeeps."

"Well, *I* don't see how come he has to find another name anyway," said Julie, leaning forward to pat Gosh's shoulder. "Joe Gosh is just *fine*," she said. "I *like* Joe Gosh!"

Gosh half turned toward her, and what do you know, she blushed.

CHAPTER

26

According to the marquee and sandwich boards in front of the Blue Robot, a chanteuse named Irene Fistick was scheduled to perform ballads of mutant love that Tuesday evening, but when Gosh, Jeeters, Julie, and Del arrived at the club, they discovered a Tandy T–I slash N seated on stage broadcasting one of Del's prerecorded stories. ". . . so I lit this gigantic cherry bomb just to scare these two good buddies of mine," said Del's voice above a tape hiss. "But right away, I tossed it in the toilet bowl. I figured, you know, that the fuse would go out. . . ."

Del winked at Gosh, then told everybody to sit down, instructed No-Deposit to take drink orders, and went off to see why the heck Irene Fistick hadn't showed.

"Your friend owns this place?" said Jeeters, scowling to his left and right, then waving a hand to dispel fallacious tobacco smoke. "What a dive."

No-Deposit returned shortly with a tray—orange Kik, all around—and as soon as he'd distributed the glasses, each one rimmed with black sugar, Julie lifted hers and proposed a toast. "To Ira and Joe," she said. "And to the Jiffy," she added, reaching across the table and clinking her glass against her brother's.

"And to obscene profits, don't forget," said Jeeters.

Gosh's fingers tightened, and his own glass exploded. That attracted more attention from the surrounding nightclubbers than it otherwise might've, because just as it happened, the storytelling robot suddenly shut up. Del, on stage, had ejected the cassette. Almost all heads turned toward Gosh, who lunged across the table and stuck his face into Jeeters's. "You can't let anybody else ride the Jiffy."

"Says who?"

"Says me."

"Baloney."

Julie said, "Guys, guys, cut it out."

And Del was saying into the stage mike, ". . . tonight's performer was unavoidably detained by the narcotics squad. However, in keeping with the Blue Robot's policy of presenting tomorrow's big stars today . . ."

"Listen," said Gosh, "I may not be the world's smartest guy—"

"No!" said Jeeters. *"Really?"*

"—but I'm smart enough to know that I'm dead in the water if the Jiffy becomes the next big consumer appliance."

Jeeters lazily probed his cheeks with his tongue, to infuriate. "You paid for a ride, you got a ride."

"Just wait six months—three months! Just wait—"

"Till you can make a little money, is that right? Till you can cash in?"

Gosh said, "Yeah." And didn't bat an eye.

"And you think *I'm* mercenary. Hey, Julie, you getting a load of this nouveau palooka? And he thinks *I'm* mercenary."

Julie had turned pale.

"You owe me some consideration, Ira."

"I do not. Where'd you get such a ridiculous idea? You're the one who came barging into my laboratory."

"Two months," Gosh pleaded. "All I'm asking you to wait is two stinking months before you say anything about the Jiffy."

"Go fly a kite."

And Del Forno, applauding wildly, exclaimed, "So without any further ado, here he is, ladies and gentlemen—Wonder City's latest wonder, Joe Gosh!"

Gosh had gripped both sides of the quartet table, and now, distressed by Jeeters's obstinance and bewildered by Del's introduction, he applied a jot of reflexive pressure. Bingo, the table split in half, and the two halves fell away, in opposite directions. Jeeters's glass toppled into his lap. Julie's hit the floor but didn't break.

A blue spot scoured the club, and finally picked out Gosh, who shielded his eyes. Then, having a sudden brainstorm, he rose from his chair, bowed modestly, and, sticking out his tongue at Jeeters, sprang into the air.

It was really neat hearing everybody gasp together.

CHAPTER

For an amateur, he was working the crowd just great.

After he'd got everyone's undivided attention with his fancy jackrabbit leap to the stage, Gosh had briefly been at a loss about what to do next. He'd stood there fidgeting with the microphone for a dreadful quarter of a minute, till, at last, Del—good old Del!—sicced a couple of bouncer-bots on him. The first hunkajunk—seven feet tall and wearing a studded bikers' cap—had clobbered his skull with a lead sap.

The blow was as damaging as a jujube.

The other robot, four-foot-nothing, broad as a jitney, and armed with a billy club, had taken a cripping whack at his left shin.

Crippling-schmippling.

Gosh smiled fatuously.

When the big robot struck him a second time, though, Gosh countered with a punch straight through its duralloy belly, his fist exiting with bits of solder and circuitry flecking his knuckles.

Out in the audience, Del Forno groaned.

Then somebody said, "Android!"

To nip that potential rumor in the bud, Gosh opened his mouth wide, then invited a young lady at a stageside table to inspect his teeth—the multitude of cheap fillings, a fresh cavity in a lower molar, coffee and tea stains, wedges of tartar.

She peered intently, then turned around and shouted to the doubting Thomas: "He's real, all right."

After that, Gosh disengaged the microphone and, giving the cord a good yank to get slack, wandered through the club like the host of a giveaway game show, maintaining a glib chatter—"How you doing? I love your chain mail. Who does your tats?"—while the Robot's patrons merrily jabbed at him with laser-shivs and cutlery. When he strolled by Jeeters and Julie—they'd moved to a new table—Jeeters said, "Very sleazy. But enjoy it while it lasts."

Julie, looking constrained and embarrassed, avoided Gosh's eye.

He completed a circuit of the club, then perched on the edge of the stage, being just-folks, and waited for The Question.

It came almost immediately, and was posed by an adenoidal guy with a shaved head and a thick blond mustache. "What the heck happened to *you,* pal?"

Narrowing his eyes and beaming victoriously at Jeeters, Gosh replied, "You remember X. S. Powers? Well, he was my dad."

CHAPTER

28

When he was a boy, Joe Gosh had wondered a great deal about his parents, of course—starting with who they were and proceeding from there. Ethnic roots, religion (if any), occupations (if applicable), native intelligence, hereditary diseases, et cetera.

And like all foundlings, he'd struggled toward self-esteem through fantasy, hatching preposterous melodramas full of intrigue, cabals, thwarted murder, and a dazzling fortune, rightfully his, to explain how come he'd ended up forsaken on the orphanage stoop.

But though his imagination was fecund, there were those black times (usually in Spanish class or during the Christmas season) when it failed utterly to spark, and he had to face the possibility that his parents had simply used up all their life credit and dropped him off on their grudging way to Mars. (Which was precisely the case. Their name was Gosch, Stan and Roedeanne Gosch, and they were still alive, burrowing away in a mole machine somewhere on the Olympus Mons. That's a whole other, sad story, though.)

By the time that Gosh was about eight years old, his gothic autobiographies had lost their appeal, and he'd begun to adopt, so to speak, real-life celebrity parents.

The first of these was a virologist from Boston named Carl Bateese, discoverer of the cure for Mosquito-Induced Nerve Disorder.

Although the war with Mars had ended before Gosh was

even born and there supposedly wasn't a single brainy mosquito left alive in the solar system, every year several hundred
thousand Earthlings had continued to succumb to a nonfatal
virus of Martian origin which left them disoriented, spastic,
and sapheaded. In popular parlance, the disease victims "lost
their MIND."

Throughout the world, the health-services cost had been
catastrophic. So, when Bateese came along with his vaccine, it
was big, splashy news. The physician quickly became everybody's darling, a Nobel laureate, a pitchman for Chevy trucks
and Coca Cola, and Joe Gosh's "dad." In daily reveries Gosh
went fishing and played catch with him, and together they
gleefully slaughtered pathogens.

Once he'd wearied of Old Man Bateese (who'd lost his
celebrity value in the real world after throttling a woman
autograph hound), Gosh took for his make-believe father a pop
singer named Gabel Bryan (big hits include: "Didn't Sleep A
Wink"; "Hap, hap, happy"; "Only Me, Only U"), and for his
mother, he selected a zaftig spacer named Carol Persaud.

In slightly under five years, Gosh adopted, then disavowed
(and the disavowals gave him nearly as much emotional pleas-
ure as the adoptions) thirteen fathers and nine mothers, all of
them solidly in the public eye.

He relished their notoriety, he was very proud of them, but
tried not to let their achievements give him a swelled head.

X. S. Powers had been slated to be Famous Dad Number
14, and no doubt would've made the best one yet—Gosh was
actually going to *meet* him! They were actually going to fly off
together! (For a few minutes, at least.) But then, great just
great, the old superman had had his fatal heart attack, ruining
everything.

After that, Gosh had soured on the Adoption Game, re-
signed himself to a weak, murky, nondescript identity, and
grew up.

Once the applause died down and the glad-handing ended,
Gosh jostled his way through the nightclub crowd, searching in

vain for Jeeters and Julie. Then Del hooked him by an elbow, spun him around, and, in a voice almost falsetto with incredulity, exclaimed, "You big fat liar!" As if he should talk, right? "What was *that* all about—inherited your father's genes!"

And Gosh broke into peals of loud, snorty laughter, feeling like a kid again.

CHAPTER

In Del's office he tossed off his filthy T-shirt, changed into a Blue Robot / Coors Beer baseball jersey (free every Wednesday evening to the first fifty customers), then left by the fire door. It was raining again. Gosh splashed down the alley and out to the sidewalk. He began to run, picking up speed and vaulting a letter box, then darting smoothly around clumps of Kik-drinking teenagers in shower caps. It was effortless, and his heart beat steadily, his breathing stayed measured, his lungs never scorched.

After a while, he cut into the street, and conceitedly raced traffic.

One hack driver really gunned it after Gosh appeared at his window, pacing the cab. They raced for almost a mile, Gosh in front, then the taxi. Gosh, taxi, Gosh, taxi. Finally, Gosh. He spurted ahead, then stopped on a corner and leaned jauntily against a lottery machine. When the cab went by at last, Gosh saluted.

Ira Jeeters made lewd gestures at him through the back window.

Gosh pushed off and ran again, zero to forty in three point five seconds. He passed the cab and kept on going.

Speed. Check.

Stamina. Check.

Can jump like a bunny. Check.

Can lift at least ten times own weight. Check.

Invulnerable. Check.

Can fly. Question mark.

Keeping up his running speed, Gosh bent his torso gradually forward and raised his arms straight out in front of him like a faith healer. Then, as he approached the great bronze statue of General Moschops treading mosquito larvae, which stood at the Fifty-first Street entrance to the city park, he leapt into the air.

He got up okay, but then the question was: How do you turn a leap into a flight?

Instinct answered before thought, and suddenly—the moment he reached zenith and felt the pull of gravity—Gosh began to kick his feet like a frogman and to do the breaststroke.

Hardly beautiful or balletic, but it worked. It worked!

Can fly. Check.

To fly, swim. It was as simple as that.

Gosh had always been a strong swimmer. Doing laps in the Soldiers and Spacers Memorial Pool was just about the only physical exercise, besides blind-dancing, that he could tolerate.

He soared, rain pelting his face, and seconds later passed into a turbulent, flickering thunderhead. Electricity skewered his brain, then jiggled out through the soles of his sneakers.

Is listed by Underwriters Laboratories, Inc. Check!

He turned, stroking powerfully with his left arm, then dove earthward. At thirty feet, he leveled off and, using telephone wires as a lap lane, breaststroked south, toward the pyramids of Hot Block.

CHAPTER

"I'm back!" Gosh yelled up the metal staircase, then went into Jeeters's lab, threw on the fluorescent lights, and sat down at a console.

It was after two in the morning, and though Gosh felt he ought to be tired, he wasn't. That worried him, vaguely. His up-and-down spirits had declined again somewhat. He'd intended to surprise Vicki Zomba when she came offstage, but when he'd arrived at Hot Block, she was already gone. The portable stage, too. The performance had been rained out.

Without touching down, Gosh had swum on toward Avenue M.

There was something he had to do, one last thing tonight. Then he could go home.

Grinning ruefully now, he got up, walked over to the Jiffy transmitter, and pulled it away from the wall. Hesitating a moment, he finally tore out some of the circuitry.

"I'm going to say this once, only once. I'm going to take a deep breath and say this one simple thing, once. Stop what you're doing right now. There!"

Julie punctuated the command with a firm nod of her head.

Gosh said, "I just need a little time. To do some concerts, sign a book deal, maybe get featured on *Other Lives to Live*. Become somebody. For just a few months. Look, this thing cost me my entire line of credit."

"Don't wreck his machine, okay? I mean, it's almost a year

of his life, okay?" She was nervous, flustered, and kept clenching her hands. "As a favor to me, all right?"

Then Jeeters came trampling in, red-faced, wearing a
short blue bathrobe and clutching a minidisk. "Julie, please
leave us alone," he bellowed, and glared at Gosh.

"Ira—I asked you nice. You're just a miserable guy." Gosh
started plucking cables.

Jeeters whacked the disk into a primitive-looking drive
and began scrabbling his fingers over an IBM keyboard.

"So you're the illegitimate son of X. S. Powers, are you?
Kept your secret all these years out of a sense of shame, did
you? All these years! I'll give you shame!"

Angrily, he jabbed Return.

Throughout Wonder City, thousands of individual pro-
grams in hundreds of supercomputers were accessed, merged,
scrambled, then wiped, so that a demon (secular readers:
substitute "malevolent entity from a synchronous universe")
that smelled powerfully like ammonia might be summoned to
the second floor of the old light-bulb factory.

CHAPTER

31

For a brief time, less than a month, when he was fifteen and a half years old, Gosh had been placed with foster parents. He was never sure what the circumstances were that had led him to become a temporary son and sibling in the Cunningham family, but whatever they were, the experience itself had been a nightmare. A nightmare.

There'd been seven Cunninghams in all, living in a condo that used to be the mail room of a magazine-publishing company. They paid thirty-eight thousand dollars a month maintenance and carrying charges. Mrs. Cunningham was a custodian at the shoe museum, and brought home a measly one thousand and nineteen devalued dollars every Friday. Mr. Cunningham was writing a novel. Naturally, the family lived mostly on credit.

So why on earth had they taken Gosh in? The social services check they'd received for his support hadn't covered by half the actual cost of feeding a hormonally active teenager.

Maybe the Cunninghams *wanted* to go bankrupt in a hurry. Maybe they'd figured life on Mars couldn't be any worse than life on Earth.

Maybe they had.

Whatever it was all about, Gosh had been miserable the whole time he was with them. The place was cramped and noisy, but worse than that, he had had to go to public school, where the doors were locked, you paid or fought for a seat, and the teachers all were licensed to stun. In the evenings, he played static-station with his foster brothers and sisters (Gosh had always hated card games) or crept through the warren of condos down past the elevators, peeking over the half-dividers, through frosted glass and keyholes, spying on the neighbors.

He'd eventually got friendly with one neighbor, Mr. Cornish, who lived at the corner, in a subdivision that once upon a time had been the company art department.

Cornish was about forty, retired from Brinks Security, and living on the fruits of some wise investments. He'd had a girlfriend who lived on another floor, in a planned community called Accountancy Acres.

Gosh had started going over there, to Cornish's place, almost every evening after his meager supper, and the three of them—Gosh, Cornish, and Maryann, the girlfriend—watched classic movies on cassettes together. They saw *Bridge Over the River Kwai*, *Gentleman with No Face*, *In Old San Francisco*, *Brave Coward Zack*, and *The Thing*.

Gosh had seen *The Thing* several times—he really liked that one—and was reminded of it now, specifically of that scene near the end where the naïve scientist tries to talk reason with a monstrous vegetable.

What reminded him was Jeeters, desperately trying to communicate with the demon he'd accessed from the void between digits. He was saying, "I'm your friend." Now, sweeping his arm around and pointing at Gosh, he said, "Enemy! En-ah-mee!"

Same as with the movie scientist, Jeeters was buffeted aside.

What did the buffeting was a tentacle, one of many, many unhealthy-looking white tentacles connected to a body that resembled a sea cow's, except for the (vaguely) human face.

It seemed almost sluggish, this thing, this demon, this malevolent entity from a synchronous universe—*until* it suddenly flung itself across the room, moving like a paper scrap in a windstorm. Tentacles lashed every which way, walloping both Jiffy stalls, smashing the wall clock, tumbling machinery galore, raising a welt on Julie's cheek, and seizing Gosh around his waist and his windpipe.

Gosh scrabbled at the chokehold, and was finally getting purchase when the demon evaporated.

After he'd gasped and was breathing again, he saw Julie, with a computer keyboard in her arms, huddled by her unconscious brother.

"Is he okay?"

"Don't talk to me, you!"

Julie wouldn't even *look* at Gosh, she just kept shaking Jeeters, roughly, by his shoulder.

At last, he came around, and the first thing he said, croaking, was: "Did it get him?"

"I sent it back, Ira. I pressed Break and sent it back."

"Why the heck did you do *that*?" he said, raising himself on an elbow.

"Yeah," said Gosh, "why'd you do that? I was just about to tear it apart. I wasn't in trouble."

Julie zinged from her crouch, standing up straight and thrusting out her chin at Gosh. "Take a hike," she said. "Just beat it, creepo. And don't come around here again!"

CHAPTER

32

"Hold on," said Shrike, "and I'll ask him." He muffled the receiver against the gray, thrumming PAC (or, personal air conditioner) slung diagonally across his bony chest. "Hey, Joseph, it's the talent coordinator at *Better Lives Than Ours*. She's offering you a segment. Eleven minutes. Film, not video-tape."

Gosh tossed down the lump of coal that he'd been trying without success to squeeze into a fabulous diamond. He'd bought three lumps of bituminous yesterday, at the Mineral and Gem Museum. They'd cost him almost eighty dollars, plus he'd had to pay a fifty-buck penalty for using cash. Seemed like a good idea, at the time. Only, he was discovering now that he wasn't nearly strong enough to apply the necessary geologic pressure. "That's a local show, isn't it?" he asked Shrike. "I'd rather do a guest spot on *Other Lives to Live*. It's network."

"Don't be so damn choosy. You're not exactly a hot tamale yet." Shrike peevishly craned an eyebrow, and said into the phone, "Can I call you back tomorrow, sweetheart? We have to check Joe's schedule a little further." Then he scowled. "Yeah? Well, *you* can stick it, too!" And slammed down the receiver. "My winning personality doesn't travel so, so . . . *winningly* on fiber-optic wire," he told Gosh. "I should concentrate more on person-to-person contact."

Gosh nodded. "Yeah, maybe you should."

Shrike's face clouded. "You criticizing me? Hey, listen, it's only been two weeks."

"Sixteen days."

"You came along at the wrong time. Is it *my* fault that Tina Megaton finally went off? It's not easy making the media do flips over a super guy with no track record when they got the destruction of Paris to play around with."

Impossible to argue with that statement, so Gosh just sighed noisily. Tina Megaton! For crying out loud!

Tina Megaton had been the world's most successful commercial terrorist. Her body one-third artificial, thermonuclear, she'd pursued a lavish international playgirl's life solely on extorted credit. For almost three years, every big-city mayor in the world had dreaded receiving one of Tina's engraved announcements, which always said the same thing: that she had checked into a swank midtown hotel under an assumed name and now wanted a cool billion to leave the metropolitan area without detonating. (Wonder City had paid her off twice.)

On the very day that Shrike had called Gosh's introductory press conference, the mayor of Paris—Audincourt or Aubusson, something with an *au*—called Tina's bluff. Bad luck! All the quickly thrown together teleobituaries for the City of Light had bollixed up Gosh's first real crack at celebrity, but good! Not a single network dispatched a camera crew—Shrike had rented an army surplus tank so that Gosh could hold it aloft in the Big Boy parking lot while he answered questions—and the two daily papers had sent only their metropolitan reporters, not the crucially important entertainment and business editors.

Instead of it being Gosh, Gosh, Gosh, it was Paris, Paris, Paris which monopolized commuter, office, and locker-room gossip. It was Paris, Paris, Paris on the lips of talk-show guests and in the snappy routines of topical stand-up comics. *Au revoir*, Paris.

Tough noogies, Gosh.

As Shrike said, he couldn't have picked a worse time to launch his career.

All told, in fifteen full days as the most powerful human being on earth, he'd racked up a measly twenty-three inches of hard copy, less than a minute of broadcast time, and just one stinking job—flying a life-saving serum three hundred miles, for which he'd received an incredibly stingy stipend of nine thousand dollars. "Take it or leave it," the public relations director at Johnson & Johnson had told Shrike over the telephone. "Beggars can't be choosers."

A few independent Hollywood producers had called, wanting to know if movie rights were still available, but so far, none had offered to draw up a letter of agreement.

Gosh had had to borrow again from Del Forno to pay the rent and the minimum due on his Only-U bill, and to buy some groceries. It was humiliating.

Shrike was working strictly on a commission basis and, for the time being, charging all expenses—for staff, letterhead stationery, postage, et cetera—to his own credit card.

It was a Thursday morning, almost ten-thirty.

As Shrike started putting in yet another phone call, Gosh said, "I thought you were going to try face-to-face persuasion for a change. Take somebody to lunch, why don't you?"

"Relax, Joseph," he said, "I know what I'm doing." Then he turned his back on Gosh and said, "Shrike Media Consultants, to speak with Congressman Bailey. Is the congressman in his office yet, honey?"

Gosh groaned, then strolled around the barrack, nodding at the cotton-candy-haired secretary who'd set up her voice-typewriter on his drawing table and was now muttering into it: ". . . this exciting young superstar can turn the most humdrum wedding reception or bar mitzvah into an unforgettable three-ring circus of astonishment. New paragraph . . ."

The ghostwriter whom Shrike had hired to do Gosh's bestseller (the very book you're reading now! Hi, Mom!) was drinking coffee in the kitchenette. He was a dour-looking, curly-haired guy in his late thirties. His baggy white T-shirt bore this legend: Shaped Experience, Inc. / Full-length Bios at Resume Rates / Novelize Your Life / Ask Me About Tax Shelters.

He watched Gosh cut a wedge out of an iced coffee cake, then said, "You have a few minutes? I'd like to get at least a few facts right." He smiled, and all his grump lines vanished.

Gosh sat down.

"You're eighteen, right?"

"Twenty."

"Eighteen, I think."

"If that's what Shrike says."

"It is."

"I'm eighteen, then."

The ghostwriter made a note of that on a tiny square of gummed notepaper, then stuck it inside a file folder.

"Do you have any pet phrases I could use in constructing dialogue?"

"Not that I'm aware of."

"Any famous young ladies in your love life, either past or present?"

"Well, I kind of have a thing going with Victoria Zomba."

"Spell it."

"Z-o-m-b-a."

"Oh, *Zomba.* The witch's daughter, you mean."

"Right."

"We bid on her mother's story, but she doesn't trust print. She signed with Listen and Listen Good. Knopf and Konopka are gonna bring out the tape at Christmas. First serial rights already sold to *Ladies Home Audio Journal.* But just what do you mean, you have *kind* of a thing with this girl? What kind of thing? Serious? Just acquainted—what?"

"Well, I guess it's almost all one-sided, but I'm in—" Gosh broke off when he saw who'd just come to the front door and was showing identification to the security guard.

Julie Jeeters!

He hadn't spoken to her since she'd thrown him out of the lab, that night of nights.

"Excuse me," he said to the writer, and almost ran to the door, amazed at how good—indeed, how thrilled—he felt just seeing her again.

She had on a snap-front denim dress with a fruit-fly pin on the jonny collar, and new white sneakers worn without socks. She'd cut and frizzed her hair. Gosh liked the way it made her face look. More worldly, somehow. Her mouth was set, unsmiling. Her eyes were concealed behind enormous red sunglasses. In her left hand she clutched a plastic shopping bag from an Italian shoe store.

"This young lady doesn't appear on Mr. Shrike's list, sir," said the guard, who happened to be that cop from the auto pound, remember him—the war veteran?

"She's a friend of mine," said Gosh.

It was the dopiest thing, having a full-time security guard on the premises, but Shrike had anticipated unruly crowds gathering in Morning Street every day to catch a glimpse of Gosh. ("Joseph," he'd finally said last evening after Gosh had once again voiced complaint, "let's just give him another week. If by next Friday there's still no big pests wanting money or favors, we'll just terminate him, okay? Okay?" And Gosh had said, "Okay." Doggone those pheromones, anyhow!)

"I'm glad you came over," Gosh said now, and Julie quirked up her mouth. "Really! I thought about calling you."

"So why didn't you?" Had her voice always been so whispery, so uninflected?

"You seemed pretty mad at me."

"You still could've called. I mean, if you'd really *wanted* to. I wouldn't've hung up." She gave a shrug, then noticed the secretary chattering into the Toshiba's condenser mike. The ghostwriter, leaning on the wet bar, saluted her with his coffee mug. "What the heck's going on here?"

"I'm trying to launch a career."

"*You* are?"

"I have some help." Gosh steered Julie by the elbow over to the sofa, and they both sat.

Shrike was watching them as he waited on hold. Then his eyes snapped and he said, "Congressman! How are you this morning? I'll make it brief, I know you have some board meetings, but I understand that you've been considering a

123

staged assassination attempt, and I think I might be able to help you maximize the impact. Get those Gallup points up."

Julie had been eavesdropping, and now she blanched. "This is not what I pictured you doing, somehow."

"Well, I haven't done *anything* yet. We're just feeling our way around. How's—how's Nippy?"

"She's all right, I guess. Pretty listless."

"Yeah? No more flying around? Or going through walls?"

She shook her head and smiled, reaching down into the shopping bag. Then she breathed heavily in annoyance, withdrew her hand, and sat back. "I'm supposed to serve you with a summons," she said, "but I can't do it. If you want it, it's in the bag. If you don't, forget about it."

"What kind of summons?"

"Ira's suing you. For breach of contract, theft of services. A bunch of other stuff."

Gosh pushed a hand across one cheek, plowing up a ridge of skin below his eyes. "Is he *serious*? That means I'm going to have to hire a lawyer. And I'm totally insolvent!"

"Relax. I'll keep saying I couldn't get near you."

"He might hire a real process-server."

"Why should he, when he's got me?" She rolled her eyes, self-deprecatingly. "So what's it like, flying around?"

Gosh shrugged. "Kind of neat. But my stomach still does flips sometimes."

"Yeah?"

"Oh, yeah. I mean, as a kid I wouldn't even walk across the Moschops Bridge. I was always scared of heights."

"Yeah, me too." She colored briefly, then shook her head. Obviously wishing to change the subject, she reached back down into her bag, with both hands this time. "I made you something," she said. "It might be inappropriate, but I thought you were, like, going into show business."

Holding it by the shoulders, she drew out a blue one-piece acrobat's leotard of compensating cotton, which meant it would provide body definition the wearer didn't naturally have—pecs, glutes, lats, et cetera. The fabric had memory woven into its fibers.

"Gee," said Gosh, "this is nice." The decorative configuration of thunderbolts on the chest was really cool. There was a little trademark patch too, analogous to the Izod alligator: it was a tiny blue heart. A valentine kind of heart, though, not the kind with auricles and ventricles. Thank goodness.

"You like it?" said Julie.

He'd only said so five times already, but he nodded emphatically and said it again. "A lot. You designed this yourself?"

"Oh, yeah."

"I thought you said you weren't that talented?"

She blushed, and Gosh was pleased with himself. It was clear she had a major crush on him, and that was tremendously flattering. Hey, the guy was still human, sort of.

He took the leotard into the bathroom and changed clothes. When he stepped back out, everyone stopped what they were doing (Shrike was tapping figures into a small calculator; the ghostwriter was making another drip-pot of coffee; the secretary was collating a printout; Julie was reading the summons she'd not delivered).

And they stared.

"So what do you think?"

Everyone said yeah, great, really great costume. Everyone except Julie. She'd spotted a couple of pieces of thread dangling around the appliqués, and as she carefully snipped them off with a tiny scissors, Shrike said, "But I don't think you should wear it *all* the time. It'd be inappropriate dress for, say, the National Manufacturers Convention."

Julie grunted under her breath.

Gosh said, "National Manufacturers?"

"Convention. In Washington, D.C.," said Shrike. "Tomorrow night. It's superhero time!"

CHAPTER

33

"Got it?"

"Yeah, I think so," said Gosh. "But if you don't mind, would you run through it just once more? I want to make *sure* I have everything straight."

The congressman's chief of staff hissed his irritation, but said, "Okay. Last time."

"Absolutely," Gosh replied, and grinned nervously. There were five other men in white dress shirts and blue ties seated around the conference table. They were in a room behind the grand ballroom of the Marriott Crystal Gateway Hotel. In twenty minutes, Congressman Bailey was scheduled to give an important address to thousands of assembled businessmen. Gosh hadn't been introduced to Bailey. Since arriving in Washington, he'd spent most of his time filling out W-4 forms and taking loyalty oaths.

"You'll be seated on stage, left of the dais," said the chief of staff.

"Right," said Gosh.

"Your cue to get ready is when the congressman announces that he's endorsing repeal of the thirteenth amendment. Get set to move."

"No problem."

"Our assassin will be in the front row. He'll be wearing a green handkerchief in his suit-coat pocket."

"Okay," said Gosh, thinking: green handkerchief, green handkerchief.

"When he jumps up, he'll say three things: *Cash only!*
That's one. *Cash in, credit out.* That's two. And, *Cash and
Carry on!* Those are his three slogans. We want to make it
clear that he's an antisocial cashist. Let him speak."

Gosh said, "I will."

"Then he fires. Just make sure you're in front of him when
he does. And you'd better be as good as your vita. Because he's
using a real raygun."

"Okay." Gosh moistened his lips. "Okay."

The chief of staff smiled and stood up from the table. His
assistants all waited a deferential moment, then also rose.
"Don't worry about a thing, it'll go great."

In fact, everything went straight to hell. The congressman
from USX was so nervous that he repeatedly stumbled over his
speech, in which he promised the gathering of businessmen
that Washington would soon be sharing its surplus of debtor
units with those industries finding it most difficult to compete
in the world market.

His tongue kept sticking to the roof of his mouth: "Non-
thalaried labah ith a thalution whoth time hath come."

Those members of the audience who understood what the
congressman was saying applauded vigorously.

He gulped from his glass of ice water.

Finally, the strain became too great and he leapt for cover,
even before he'd spoken his key words.

The planted assassin, utterly confused, fired without de-
claiming his cashist slogans.

He squeezed off two pulses from an AT&T heater, and the
speaker's podium burst into flames.

Gosh flung himself off the stage and into the front row,
coming down on top of the assassin just as his heater flashed
again.

Gosh screamed.

CHAPTER

34

"Achilles," said Del. "I must've been absent at school that day. Refresh my memory."

"The Greek hero. His mother dipped him in this magic water and nothing could hurt him afterward? Except for his heel. His heel could be hurt. Come on, Del: Achilles."

"Never heard of him. But wait a second. Why his heel? You mean, like, the heel of his *foot*?"

"Of course his foot. It's where his mother held him, see? So it didn't get wet."

"I don't buy that. *It didn't get wet!* Baloney. If I held your wrist and we both stuck our hands in a sink full of water, you're gonna tell me your *wrist* wouldn't get wet? Get off my case."

"It's only a *story,* Del."

"Oh—it's only a *story*! You didn't say that." He was quiet for a long moment, then said, "So how come your eyeballs got burnt?"

"Because I *shut* them in the Jiffy."

"You think?"

"It makes sense."

"Does it?"

"Well, it's the only explanation *I* can come up with."

Del shrugged. Then: "How many fingers am I holding up?"

"Three."

"You're gonna be fine."

Gosh nodded, almost believing it. He *could* see Del's

fingers, though as smeary silhouettes. All he could make out of Del's face, though, was his mouth. The rest of it was pretty vague.

After the fiasco in D.C., he'd been totally sightless for three days. But for a week now he'd been able to see a little bit, every day a little bit more. For a while, though, man. Whew!

His terror at being handicapped had been mitigated somewhat by the dozens of interviews he'd given.

Society was definitely starting to get interested in Joe Gosh. You bet! Already, he'd been on television, three times—as a panelist on a prime-time game show, as a witness at a congressional subcommittee hearing called to investigate the attempted assassination, and as the Personality Pick of the Week on *Other Lives to Live*.

Not bad, right?

After each appearance, though, Shrike had criticized him: "Don't swallow your words so much. And stop saying *um*, would you?"

Shrike had ordered a thousand glossy photos and an autograph machine.

"You looked real good on television," Del Forno was saying now. "I taped everything, so you don't have to feel bad. When you can see again, you can watch yourself till you puke."

"How could I've looked good? Maybe if I was an old-time blues singer, I would've looked good. I had on *blindman's* glasses!"

"You did not. You had on aviator goggles."

"What?"

"Aviator goggles. Shrike gave you aviator goggles. You're wearing them right now, as a matter of fact."

Astounded, Gosh clapped his hands to his face, and his fingers went tapping around the bug lenses. "Hey!"

"They make you look tough." Del chuckled. "And Julie's costume looked nifty." Immediately, he fell silent, and Gosh could sense his awkwardness. "How many fingers," Del said half a minute later.

"Have you seen her?"

"How many fingers?"

"Get out of here, with your fingers. You've seen Julie, haven't you?"

"We just went to the movies together. It was that horror movie everybody's talking about. *Freaks Amok.* It wasn't worth the price of hypnosis."

"How's she doing?"

"Don't ask me that in that tone of voice, Joey. She's not your girfriend or anything."

"I'm just asking. I didn't think I was using any special tone of voice."

"Well, you were. Now—*how many fingers?*"

Gosh went to slap Del's hand out of his face. But at the last instant, he checked himself. He could've shattered his buddy's intercarpal, or something. Which, come to think of it, maybe he should've done.

He didn't like it one bit, Del's going out with Julie Jeeters. Not one tiny little bit.

Gosh was down, down in the dumps.

CHAPTER

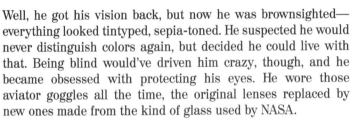

Well, he got his vision back, but now he was brownsighted—everything looked tintyped, sepia-toned. He suspected he would never distinguish colors again, but decided he could live with that. Being blind would've driven him crazy, though, and he became obsessed with protecting his eyes. He wore those aviator goggles all the time, the original lenses replaced by new ones made from the kind of glass used by NASA.

He even slept in the stupid goggles.

Which meant he had to sleep on his back.

This morning he lay in a strange bed staring at the room sprinkler on the ceiling.

He was in a motel thirty miles south of Chicago. Yesterday, he'd flown out here to help untangle a train wreck, spent all afternoon lifting boxcars out of a muddy creek and lugging them up a grade of cinders, then setting them down on transport-carriers.

The money was good, the coverage excellent.

This afternoon he was catching a one o'clock flight back to Wonder City. No way could he fly that far by himself. What, six hundred miles? No way. Could he *swim* six hundred miles? Besides, there was too much air traffic. And besides *that,* he probably would've gotten lost.

Finally, he forced himself out of bed, and dressed. Then, taking his portable press from his luggage, he ran his Only-U card through it, to check his balance. Because he'd made an extra payment against his outstanding balance last night, using his advance from the train job, he now had twenty thousand dollars in available credit. Deduct the costs of the flight back home and the motel room—nine thousand and some-odd bucks—and that still left him with a little over ten thousand. He decided he could spring for breakfast in the coffee shop.

On the way there along the corridor, weaving around maid's carts full of sheets and pillowcases, he was hailed by a chauffeur in livery. "Your limousine is outside, Mr. Gosh," he said.

Gosh panicked. He couldn't afford a limousine! He'd planned to take the motel's courtesy bus to the airport. "I'm sorry," he said. "But I haven't ordered a car."

"But the Foundation did, sir."

"The Foundation?"

"The National Scions Foundation. Now, if you'll just come with me. Their plane is waiting."

"I'm going to Wonder City."

"So is the plane."

Gosh flicked an eyelash hair off one of the goggle lenses, then shrugged and said, "Well, I have to check out first."

"I've already taken that liberty."

"Yeah? Well, I have to cancel my flight."

"And I've taken that liberty, as well."

Gosh went back to his room and got his suitcase.

The little rich boy's name was Eric, and he kept referring to Ma Zomba as Mommy.

"Mommy says you're coming to Brazil with us."

And: "Mommy says if we don't find that guy, we shouldn't bother to come back, none of us!"

And: "I wish Mommy wouldn't act so mean."

Gosh turned a sour look on Eric, who was seated across from him on the plane, thirty thousand feet over Toledo at the moment. They each occupied an enormous leather sofa. Gosh glanced away, through the window at the clouds, which resembled floes of arctic ice. "I don't know anything about going to Brazil," he said.

"Mommy says."

"I don't care what Mommy says."

"But Mommy *says!*"

Gosh sighed, watching the clouds go by.

From the Moschops Airport, which served Wonder City and the greater metropolitan sprawl, Gosh was driven in a pink limo to the Several Acres Country Club. At the gate, a uniformed guard, blinky and slow-talking, said that the club was closed that afternoon for a private party. Eric cranked down his window and said, "We're expected! We're *guests,* you potbrain! Eric Forchune and Joseph Gosh!"

The guard checked a list on his clipboard, then apologized and touched the visor of his cap.

"Stupid potbrain!" said Eric as they were rolling up the drive.

Gosh noticed a lot of young zombies standing very still all across the golfing fairway, some playing in the sand trap.

"We're going to see Mrs. Zomba?' he asked.

"Who do you think we're gonna see—the Commissioner of Baseball?"

"Oh, shut up, Eric."

Gosh was reminded of doggerel popular when he was a kid:

> Rich girls go to Mars to become movie stars
> Rich boys go to Jupiter to become stupider

He chuckled to himself, but stopped chuckling when the chauffeur suddenly swerved the limo off the graveled roadway and drove it straight across the freshly barbered lawn to the edge of the swimming pool.

Even before he got out of the car, Gosh saw that the pool was filled with several varieties of shark, mantas, and swordfish, all of them gliding quietly just below the surface of the turquoise waters.

From loudspeakers mounted on lampposts and cabana roofs, the Honky Tonk Man's version of "Detroit City" was playing.

"We'll stick around to drive you back to the airport," Eric said.

"I'm not *going* back to the airport."

"Yes you are."

"No I'm not.

"That's what *Mommy* says!"

Gosh gave it up, got out, and slammed the car door. A white-jacketed waiter appeared at his elbow. "If you'd care for a dip, sir, I can get you a suit and a low-powered laser. The party theme, as you can see, is aquarium life."

"No, thank you," said Gosh, standing at poolside, watching

a manta glide over the fluke of a small black whale, then speed up, passing a sand shark.

The shark lunged at the manta, and instinctively Gosh flinched and stepped backward on blue slate. The ray skedaddled, and the shark cut diagonally across the pool toward the aluminum ladder, its beady eyes as dead as coat buttons.

As the shark climbed out, it turned misty and became Ma Zomba. Water crashed off her blubbery shoulders. She squeezed out her hair, then unbelted the laser projector and flipped it away underhand—it landed on a stack of red Styrofoam kickboards.

Her swimsuit was skirted, and the balloon motif would've been more appropriate on a garment made for a six-year-old.

But even in such a getup, she could still intimidate Gosh.

Over the loudspeaker, the Honky Tonk Man was singing "Six Days on the Road." *And I'm a-gonna make it home tonight.*

"Is Vicki in there?" Gosh asked Ma.

"She's the manta, there."

"Is she? Is she really?" Gosh bent over and peered.

Ma squeezed his forearm with her wet hand, pulling him toward an umbrella table. "I want to talk to you."

"About Brazil?"

"That, and a few other things."

They sat, and the waiter scurried over. "Something to drink?" said Ma.

"Do you have lemon Kik?" Gosh asked the waiter.

"Kik!" said Ma. "Oh, grow up, Joe Gosh." She turned to the waiter. "We'll both have diet Pepsis."

He went away, and Ma sat back in her seat.

Gosh looked at the lifeguard's throne. A couple of zombies in beige pith helmets were up there playing 500 rummy with gravity cards.

"You can look at me," said Ma. "I won't pull any mischief, I promise."

Still, Gosh sat sideways on the chair with his legs crossed, glancing at Ma every few seconds. "So what's all this Brazil stuff?" he said. "I already know about the expedition. But I can't stand humidity. I'm not going into any jungle."

"If you bring back the Honky Tonk Man, you can name your reward."

"Hey, what is this, the Bible? You can't just promise me your daughter in marriage."

"Is that your price?"

The Pepsis came then, and Gosh used the interruption to skip answering that particular question.

Ma apparently decided not to press him. She slid the wrapper off her drinking straw, rolled it into a ball, and said, "How'd you manage the great transformation?"

"I was *always* this way. I just chose to live an ordinary life. Till now. You know how kids are—they don't want to be different."

Ma blew out breath. "Yeah, yeah," she said. "But just between you and me, what's the *real* story?"

Gosh smiled at her, then glanced off again, just as one of the helmeted zombies tossed up the playing cards. All the suits tumbled into orbits around their respective aces.

Then something else caught Gosh's eyes: the manta ray slithering over the side of the pool, flickering into Vicki Zomba.

Ma stood up. "Well, I'll just leave you two kids alone."

Vicki glided across the flagstones, water beading on her sunblock.

The Honky Tonk Man was singing "Waltz Across Texas."

CHAPTER

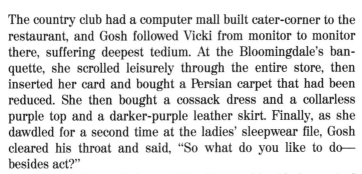

The country club had a computer mall built cater-corner to the restaurant, and Gosh followed Vicki from monitor to monitor there, suffering deepest tedium. At the Bloomingdale's banquette, she scrolled leisurely through the entire store, then inserted her card and bought a Persian carpet that had been reduced. She then bought a cossack dress and a collarless purple top and a darker-purple leather skirt. Finally, as she dawdled for a second time at the ladies' sleepwear file, Gosh cleared his throat and said, "So what do you like to do—besides act?"

"Shop." She smiled up at him. He stood beside her swivel chair and smiled back.

"And besides that?"

"Um—I like keeping track of our investments."

Deciding that this line of conversation wasn't leading anywhere, Gosh asked, "Are you still in that musical?"

"*Vixen of Venice?* No, that's over. I think I'd like to do a movie next. I've done TV, I've done theater, film is the logical next step. My mother is still checking out producers."

Gosh suppressed a smile. I'll bet she is! he thought. Look into my eyes and repeat after me: Vicki Zomba is star material.

"Maybe you can be in *my* movie," Gosh said.

"You're making a movie?" Suddenly he was more interesting than lace-edged camisoles.

"Well, the details aren't all worked out yet. But I'm definitely being optioned." Pure fantasy.

"That's great!" said Vicki. "But what kind of part could I play?"

"You could play yourself."

"That's not much of a role."

"Not now, maybe."

She laughed. "Boy, do we sound sophisticated."

"Really," Gosh agreed, and they wandered down the mall together, in silence.

Then, at the same time, Gosh said, "How come your mother—" and Vicki said, "How'd you get your pow—"

"Excuse me," said Gosh.

"No, you first."

"I was going to ask you how come your mother is so crazy to find the Honky Tonk Man? She doesn't want him for *you*, does she?"

"Not for me, silly, for her! He's her *husband*. He's, like, my *father*."

"Are you serious?"

"It's all in my mother's autobiography, which is coming out on cassette in a few months. She reveals the whole story for the first time. The secret courtship, the midnight wedding, all that stuff."

"But you haven't answered my question. Are you *serious*? Or is she just saying that to get a bestseller?"

Vicki got in a snit. "My mother is already more wealthy than you can imagine. She doesn't care about having a bestseller. She just wants to set the record straight. All those other women claiming *they* were married to the Honky Tonk Man are just plain liars. So I've answered *your* question. Now you answer *mine*. How'd you get your superpowers?"

Gosh said, "My father was X. S. Powers."

"So how come your name is Gosh, which, by the way, is a pretty stupid one."

"Gosh was my mother's name. She wasn't married. Look, I don't like to talk about it. It's still kind of a raw subject."

After turning a severe, darkly skeptical look on him, Vicki

suddenly smirked and said, "Maybe when you come back from Brazil, we could go out dancing. You blind-dance?"

"Oh, yeah."

"So maybe when you come back."

"I'm not sure that I'm going."

"Oh, I bet you do," she said, and pushed through a fire door into bright late-afternoon sunlight. She ran off across the lawn, toward the pool, where a porpoise was leaping out of the water and into the air and becoming a muscle-bound young man.

As she dove off the low board, turning manta again, Eric and his chauffeur rolled up beside Gosh in a golf cart. "You about ready to leave?" Eric asked him.

"I don't have a passport."

"You don't need one, sir," said the chauffeur. "You've been designated a Citizen of the World."

"Me?" Citizen of the World? Cowabunga! "How the heck did you manage that?"

"Not me, sir," said the chauffeur. "Mommy."

1 4 1

CHAPTER

On the flight to Rio, Gosh was constantly bothered by noisome little boys in Abercrombie safari suits. They all wanted him to *do* something, like smash himself in the head with a hammer, or something. Finally, just to get a little peace and quiet, he asked the steward for a knife and tried to plunge it into his carotid artery. It broke—the knife, not the artery—and then the boys wanted Gosh to do something *else*. It was a very trying, very long flight.

They came into Galeao Airport, and after passing unchecked through customs, Gosh and the boys were met by an Irish soldier of fortune named Tumulty, who would be leading the jungle trek. Tumulty was fat-necked and thick-bodied and crewcut; his face was sunburnt. He was wearing a camouflage shirt and surfer jams. He had a music bug in one ear, and a PAC snug in an armpit, where you might expect to find a gun in a holster. Macho to a fault, he treated the boys scornfully, but took a shine to Gosh, or appeared to.

Riding in Tumulty's black auto to the hotel, they passed a long white beach teeming with exhibitionist bathers.

"During the last revolution in Nicaragua," Tumulty said to Gosh, "I used to read a lot, between skirmishes. I read a book called *Powers That Be*. You ever read that one?"

"No."

"It was supposedly the autobiography of that guy X. S. Powers. But I don't guess he actually wrote it."

"Probably not."

"Anyhow. In that book, he presented himself as a pretty upright-living guy. So I'm glad you came along to sully his memory." Tumulty grunted, then opened his mouth and smiled. His teeth were preposterously large. "I hate people that make themselves out to be so great. Everybody's corrupt, everybody's a phony. Some people just hide it better than others. Don't you think?"

Gosh moved his head noncommittally. This Tumulty character gave him the creeps.

"Have all the preparations been made?" Gosh asked, to steer the conversation away from misanthropy.

"Yeah, everything's ready to go. I've put together a good solid team. If that Honky Tonk hillbilly is still alive, we'll find him."

"Let's hope it doesn't take too long."

"If you get bored," said Tumulty, "you can just uproot some trees. You might even be able to earn a few extra bucks from the Brazilian government. They pay a nice bounty for jungle bashing."

"Yeah? Really?"

"Sure. Every cleared acre of jungle is one more grazing acre for hamburger cows."

They sped along the highway, Gosh ogling the girls of Ipanema beach.

"Wow," said Julie, "Rio de Janeiro! It must be costing you a fortune to call me. But please don't go into arrears on my account."

Gosh said, "I'm charging this to somebody else's card."

Eric's. Eric, himself, was ensconced in Gosh's suite—at the moment sprawled on the carpet, watching television.

"So how you doing, Julie?"

"I'm okay. When're you coming back?"

"I don't really know. This trip was all very sudden."

"Sounds like it."

"Listen, could you do me a big favor? Could you go over to my place tomorrow and tell Shrike where I am? Tell him not to arrange any more interviews or jobs or stuff for me while I'm gone, okay? Would you?"

"Why don't you tell him yourself?"

"I can't call *everybody*. I'm leaving in the morning for the Amazon!"

"Don't get snarky. I just think you're dumping on me, is all. Now I have to run around doing errands for you, too?"

"Just this once?"

"Is that the only reason why you called?"

"No," said Gosh, "of course not."

"Why didn't you call Vicki Zomba? I mean, if you *had* to call somebody."

"How do you know about her?"

"Delbert told me. So why *didn't* you call her?"

Gosh frowned. "I didn't—"

He nearly said, "—want to," but at the last instant, he chickened out and said, "—have her number."

Thousands of miles away on the North American continent, Julie Jeeters hung up.

"Hey!" said Eric just then, "you should see!" He was pointing at the television screen, gesturing with a Hershey bar. "This is a riot. This is *wild! Baron Mencken's Wonderland* in *Portuguese!*"

Son of a gun. Eric wasn't kidding. The world's worst syndicated children's program had, somehow, gotten itself on Brazilian television!

Gosh sat down on the edge of the bed and watched Vicki Zomba as Lady Sunny-Weather show Squirrely how to affix a postal stamp to an envelope. And even though her voice was strange, incomprehensible, *dubbed,* he was as entranced as ever, damn it!

CHAPTER

Gosh flew ahead of the boat, sometimes soaring—from up high, the Amazon River looked like a brown thread in a green carpet—and sometimes just skirting the surface of the water. If he'd wanted to, he could've reached a hand down and brushed his fingertips over crocodiles, grabbed an electric eel, been sucker bait for piranha. Man, it was hot and sticky! And the mosquitoes were so thick you couldn't help swallowing a few every time you breathed. Occasionally, some poison-tipped arrows came whistling out of the reeds, and plinked harmlessly off our hero's impervious hide.

This was the third full day out on the river.

Finally, Gosh tired of playing scout and returned to the deck of the boat—an air-conditioned, needle-prowed white yacht. A few of Tumulty's men were leaning on the rail, using revolvers to take potshots at giant catfish. They eyed Gosh suspiciously. He went belowdeck into the lounge, where the little boys were gathered around a projection screen watching a movie on laser disc.

The movie was *Country Jungle,* and it happened to be the very last movie made by the Honky Tonk Man; in fact, he'd disappeared while filming it, which explained why you kept seeing the back of the HTM's head so much. They'd had to use a stand-in to complete a lot of scenes.

As Gosh poured himself a lemonade, he watched a bit of it. The Honky Tonk Man looked handsome, and muscle-bound in a white polo shirt. The character he was playing was named

Deke Blakely, an innocent man on the run. In the story, he was hiding out on a rubber plantation. The boss man's beautiful daughter from Ohio arrives one day for a visit. Naturally, she goes crazy for the Honky Tonk Man. He's so—exciting, so mysterious! And so quiet, except for when he sings sad songs by the campfire.

One of the scions said, "That actress who's playing the daughter? She was my father's third wife. She's not my mother, though. My father's fifth wife is my mother."

The other boys shushed him up, so as not to be distracted from the great scene where the Honky Tonk Man rescues the girl from a lion.

"There aren't any lions in the Amazon jungle!" exclaimed the boy who'd been silenced. "Hey, Joe—are there lions in the Amazon, in real life?"

Gosh shrugged. He didn't know. (There aren't.)

After the Honky Tonk Man saved the girl, a native dressed in a loincloth made of palm fronds suddenly appeared with a twelve-string guitar. He played, and the HTM sang "Blue Eyes Crying in Rain."

Gosh went up the staircase to the pilot house.

"Just the man I want to see," said Tumulty when Gosh walked in. "Listen, we're going to reach base camp in another hour. Then we're going to have to hoof it."

Nodding, Gosh said, "There're no paths or anything? It's all just—jungle?"

Tumulty grinned mirthlessly. "No paths."

Gosh gnawed on a thumbnail. "This guy disappeared almost twenty years ago! He could've walked to the Arctic Circle in all *that* time!"

"Well," said Tumulty, "for sure. Or he could've been swallowed by a snake. Which brings me to what I wanted to talk to you about. Let me run this past you, see what you think. We could get all tired and sweaty and diseased looking for this guy, *or* we could get comfortable in this hacienda that I know about and just hold the boys for ransom. They're all worth about ten billion apiece. What do you think?"

Gosh looked out the window, at a tribe of howler monkeys frenetic in the treetops. Then he scoured the backs of his teeth with his tongue. Then he glanced over at Tumulty. "We get tired and sweaty and diseased, understand?"

Tumulty snorted in disgust. "That's easy for you to say!"

Gosh smiled. Yeah. Yeah, it was.

CHAPTER

Standing at the site where the Honky Tonk Man had last been seen was a brass tablet—erected long, long ago, judging from the way it was overgrown with flowering vines. Gosh tore enough away so that he could read the inscription. "We Shall Never Forget You," it read. At the bottom right-hand corner it read "Honky Tonk Man International Fan Club / Audrey Zomba, President."

Tumulty was shouting, "Let's get up the tents, men! Somebody make a fire. Somebody shoot those monkeys!"

Hundreds of monkeys, the organ-grinder kind, had gathered to watch the goings-on, and the chattering racket they made was deafening. And they kept throwing nuts at everybody! "Ow!" said Eric, rubbing his head. Then he turned to Gosh and said, "Can't you make them stop?"

Gosh said, "What do I look like, the building superintendent?"

But the monkeys just kept it up and kept it up, and no matter how many rounds Tumulty fired at the tribe, they wouldn't be quiet or quit beaning everybody with nuts. It was impossible to sit around the campfire, so finally the boys went to their swank tent, and Tumulty and his men retired to army-surplus ones, leaving Gosh outside by himself. Even though he was constantly pelted, he didn't feel a thing, and he'd plunged so deeply into thought that he no longer even heard the monkeys' gibbering.

He was thinking about his new career, and what to make of it. Everything had happened so quickly that he hadn't had much time before now to consider what his powers actually might *mean*, and how they might, well, *cost* him. He'd already damaged his eyesight because he hadn't been careful. If he didn't watch out, something even worse could happen.

Such as?

All right: what about his ears? (Don't laugh.) How deep, he wondered, did his skin armoring extend? Were his inner ears vulnerable to damage? He was already wearing eye goggles twenty-four hours a day—should he be wearing earplugs, as well?

And take a simple thing like an appendectomy. What if his appendix should burst? How could he get an operation?

Look at what happened to X. S. Powers!

Then Gosh's anxiety really opened up, and the misgivings poured out like Greeks from the Trojan horse.

So he had super this and super that, strength, stamina, and so on. So what? What could he *do* with all that stuff, really? He was disqualified from professional sports; just the other day, Shrike had had a long conversation with the commissioner of the National Football League. So, sports were out, and he didn't want to go into the military. Maybe he should try to land a security job at US Biscuit or Dyne Robotics, someplace like that.

But what happens, he thought, when Ira Jeeters builds another Jiffy, when there's suddenly a *glut* of superpowered people in the world? What happens then, huh?

The first fish that survived on land must've been a pretty big shot for a while, but once there were *dozens* of amphibians, *thousand, millions*—why, that original superfish must've found himself just another slob again.

Is *that* what this is all leading to? Gosh asked himself.

In six months, will I be just another slob again?

On my way to Mars?

They couldn't *make* me go! How could they *make* me?

They couldn't, *could they?*

Gosh shoved that question aside, and thought instead about Ira Jeeters.

And felt a pang of guilt for having *almost* wrecked the Jiffy.

(The demon did it *really,* not me!)

And then he was thinking about Vicki Zomba, and about how difficult a time he'd had just finding something to *say* to her.

Then he thought of Julie.

Then he thought of Julie and Del.

And then he tossed back his head and exhaled in irritation.

While his head was still tipped back, he glanced up into a tree and saw a long-haired, naked male crouched on a bough, a shaft of moonlight diagonally striping his hairy chest.

Terror-stricken capuchin monkeys fled higher into the foliage as Gosh clambered up the white trunk and onto a branch, balanced himself and set off clumsily after the figure he'd seen. The Jiffy had improved his physical coordination a hundredfold, but even so, he wasn't as nimble as the activity demanded. Half a dozen times, moving from branch to branch, from tree to tree, he lurched and nearly toppled into space.

Eventually, the naked person caught a vine and shinnied down. Gosh simply jumped. His impact, though, drove three inches of sloughy grass around his ankles. The few seconds that he wasted extracting himself were enough for the figure to vanish.

No—not completely!

Gosh spotted a grayish blur behind the tentacular roots of a dead tree lying on its side, but when he reached the spot— nobody! So he braced a foot against the tree and pushed. It rolled over, to reveal a hole in the ground, a passable crevice.

Gosh stood there and looked at it.

No way.

No way he was crawling in *there*!

No fricken way.

He turned around and went back to camp.

CHAPTER

Along with machetes and rifles and Spam and such, the expedition had come provisioned with a crate of transistorized ash hounds, and several cowboy shirts that until very recently had been on display at the Country Music Hall of Fame, in Nashville, Tennessee.

When Gosh stepped out of his tent next morning, he found Tumulty running a special mini vacuum cleaner over one of the shirts. He was collecting body ash, minuscule pieces of skin that had flaked off the Honky Tonk Man and settled into the shirt cotton years ago. In all, Tumulty vacuumed four separate shirts, and when he had enough ash, he used a crowbar to break open the crate full of ash hounds.

With their legs unfolded, the hounds stood as tall as, and were as long as, full-grown German shepherds. They were sleek and shiny with triangular heads, and were menu-driven.

R-R-R-

RUFF! MY NAME IS DEVIL. INSERT OPERATING SYSTEM WHEN READY.

The hounds were all quickly programmed, and a thimbleful of Honky Tonk Man body ash tapped into each of their analyzer ports.

"Before we start out," said Gosh, "could one of those dogs give a quick sniff to that tree over there?"

"Why?" asked Tumulty.

So Gosh told him about the naked guy.

"Hey, wouldn't *that* be convenient," said Tumulty. "Wouldn't it be great if he was right around here all the time."

Gosh lifted the metal dog into the tree.

It didn't detect any matching body ash, but it did take a sudden swipe at one of the teasing monkeys, and nearly slashed its belly open with a razor paw.

"Let's move out," said Tumulty.

The ash hounds went first, then Gosh, then everybody else, in single file.

So if it hadn't been the Honky Tonk Man last night, who?

They saw a lot of tree snakes that morning, and some of the largest rodents in the world.

But no lions, which pleased Gosh.

The hounds digested particles of jungle dust by the quadrillions, but found nothing that matched the Honky Tonk Man's body ash, until the afternoon of the fourth day.

By then, the boys were all cranky and truculent, whining that their feet ached or that their PAC's had cut off, or just that this was *boring, boring,* too boring for *words.* "When are we gonna go home?" they asked, over and over. "Are we gonna go home soon?"

Tumulty's mercenaries regarded them with utter scorn.

The porters joked about them in their native tongue.

Gosh had begun to fear that this all might end badly.

What if Tumulty decided to abandon the manhunt and go for the really big bucks? What if he decided to snatch the boys for ransom, regardless of what Gosh had said?

Gosh wasn't worried about himself (not much, anyway), but he didn't want the kids to get hurt, or killed.

He'd been feeling edgy about things for the last twenty-four hours, so it was a great, great relief when the hounds suddenly started beeping and dinging their positive readings.

"We'll make camp here tonight," said Tumulty, shrugging his knapsack off a shoulder. "Maybe we're gonna find this sucker, after all."

"I hope so," said Gosh.

After dinner, deviled ham on white again, he went into his

tent and, for the first time, sat down to write in the blank journal that he'd bought in Rio.

Here I am (he wrote), *up the river (ha ha). It's really hot, but I guess it's beautiful and for sure it's an adventure.*

Then he couldn't think of anything else to write, so he doodled a few dinosaurs.

He was still sitting there, sketching with a fiber-tip pen, when he heard a buzzing sound outside, and several rifle shots.

Then a mosquito stylet as long as a cavalry saber tore through the tent's canvas roof.

CHAPTER

42

No doubt about it: Gosh had never been more frightened in his life; this even beat, hands down, that time three guys held him up at knife point and stole the music bug right out of his ear.

He jumped up from the cot, no thought in his head except to escape through the tent flap. But the mosquito—it was a female, hungry for a blood meal—dove at him, wings humming like a model-train transformer. She encircled his waist with mandibles that could've crushed a Buick. Then she poked at his shoulder, trying to puncture it.

Gosh was so grossed out that he reacted slowly. But when he finally did struggle and break free, he tore off the mosquito's maxillae by accident, then he deliberately tore out her proboscis.

She fell over, squirting and oozing.

He flung open the flap, and outside was a scene from a big-budget monster movie. Eight or nine adult mosquitoes, their bodies parallel to the ground, their bristly abdomens heaving, were sipping blood from a like number of Tumulty's men—and Tumulty himself—who'd been stung into insensibility.

The porters had all fled.

The scions' tent had been slashed to ribbons; its side hung open like a slice of turkey roll. But the boys? There was no sign of them, either.

A spindly-legged male mosquito stood lookout on an outcrop of rock at the perimeter of the campsite. It lifted its head now, and as soon as it noticed Gosh, its wings vibrated and it rose, wobbling, into the air.

Gosh stepped clear of his tent and planted himself, almost in a wrestler's crouch.

He still couldn't believe this. Mosquitoes from Mars! But, but—but they were all supposed to have been *annihilated,* years ago!

Hey, guys! The war is over! You lost!

The mosquito was hovering about six feet above Gosh now, shifting its balance, its long, slender, scaly body rising in back. It was definitely going to attack, and Gosh was ready. Skeeved out, but ready.

Then a loud ululating whistle, really a weird sound, suddenly filled the moist air, causing a shudder to pass through the male mosquito; all the females looked up from their nutrients.

Gosh risked a sidelong glance, and saw, posed like a municipal statue in the branch of a hardwood tree, a naked man with long, long graying black hair. He pursed his lips and made that whistling sound a second time.

On a branch on the other side of the same big tree stood a teenaged boy, also long-haired, also naked.

The boy, who was equipped with a bow and a quiver of arrows, said, "Tell 'em if they don't go right now, Daddy, I'm gonna start picking them off."

"Shut up," said the Honky Tonk Man.

CHAPTER

"No fooling, he's still famous?" said Junior.

"Well, his music still gets played."

"Hey, Daddy, you hear that? Your music still gets played."

The Honky Tonk Man lifted a shoulder in a couldn't-care-less kind of shrug. Now that the mosquitoes had gone, at his command, he was mixing up mud, shaking water from a canteen, and stirring the dirt with his finger; he slopped some on Tumulty and his men. Their mosquito bites were as big as carbuncles.

"It was you that I saw last night, wasn't it?" said Gosh.

Junior nodded, then asked, "You came here just to look for my daddy? That's how come you came? For no other reason?"

"Well, not *just* to find him. We're supposed to bring him back with us."

Junior twisted his mouth to one side. His eyes were black and his skin was a pinkish-copper color. He was about fifteen or sixteen years old; his complexion was as smooth as a very young girl's. "He won't go back witchoo."

"I could overpower him. I think that's how come Ma Zomba sent me along."

Junior's eyes widened slightly.

"So you've heard of her?" said Gosh.

"The lady whose name is on that plaque? Oh, sure, I've heard stories about *her*, all right." Then Junior said, "But what do you mean, overpower him? I don't think so, Moe."

Gosh didn't reply immediately. He was looking away from

Junior, seeing, to his great relief, Eric and Eric's fellow board members come sheepishly out of the rain forest, where they'd fled during the mosquito attack.

"Who are those little fellas?" Junior asked.

"No, really," said Gosh, "I can just *make* him go, whether he wants to or not."

Junior said, "*I* might be interested in going, though."

And Eric, ogling Junior and his father, said, "Hey, neat, a couple of Tarzans!"

Eventually, a few of the porters wandered back to camp (about a dozen of them never did show up again), and everybody, not including Tumulty and his still-dazed mercs, got busy undoing the shambles the mosquitoes had made. Once the tents were back up and mended with Velcro patches, it was almost dark, so Gosh built a big fire, to burn the insect that he'd killed. As he and Junior lugged the carcass to the flames, Gosh pompously said, "See how I demolished this baby? All I'd have to do to your father is tap him on the head, he'd be out like a light. You, too."

Junior smiled, then together they heaved the diptera onto the bonfire. She crackled and fizzed, and burned as quickly as wood shavings. The flames made hectic shadows on Junior's face. "I think I mean it, about going back witchoo. If you'll take me."

"No problem," said Gosh, "but the old man goes, too. Is he"—Gosh looked around, spotted the HTM squatted by himself just this side of the tree line—"a little funny in the head, or something?"

Earlier, when Gosh had introduced himself, the Honky Tonk Man had grunted, wiped off his muddy hands on his belly, and walked away.

"He's fine," said Junior. "He's just wondering what he should do with all you fellas, I guess. See, he's got no intention of being found, ever. He likes it here. It reminds him of Georgia."

"But not you? You don't like it?"

"Every day is pretty much like the one before, you know? And there're no girls."

"Really?"

"You see any? There's just him, me, and my mother." Then he said, "I can't believe that that Zomba woman sent you. According to Daddy, she made his life miserable. She used to say she'd kill him, if he didn't marry her."

"I thought they *were* married."

"Are you kidding? Don't let Daddy hear you say that. She was just another screwball that fell in love with his records. Only, she was screwier than the rest. She'd try anything to make him love her. Sent him tons of letters, made tons of threats, once she even kidnapped him. Oh, Daddy used to tell us some stories about *her*! The only thing she never tried was, was" —he struggled for something hyperbolic to say— "black magic!"

Gosh smiled to himself. So Ma hadn't always been a hoodoo queen, he thought, and wondered where, and when, she'd picked up her skills. "A real pest, she sounds like."

It was hard imagining Ma Zomba as a lovesick girl.

"Oh, she was a pest and a half, Daddy says."

"Is that why he ran away into the jungle? To get away from her?"

Junior gave Gosh a cockeyed look. "He didn't *run away* into the *jungle*. They were making this *really* crummy movie, and Daddy just got tired of hanging around one day and took a walk. Then he couldn't find his way back, and then—" Junior stopped abruptly.

Tumulty had just winced to his feet, and was gingerly prodding the edges of his whopper mosquito bite with his fingertips. But then he sat down again, curled up on the ground, and went to sleep.

"And *then* what happened?" said Gosh, urging Junior on.

Several of the scions were roasting wieners over the bonfire.

"It's a long story," said Junior.

The Honky Tonk Man unfolded himself from his stoop and

strode across the campsite, and when he reached Gosh, he hooked him by an arm and walked him hurriedly into the jungle, as grim-faced as a peace officer escorting a prisoner to arraignment.

"Let us get two things straight, sonny boy," he said. "One, I'm not going anywhere. And two, I heard you talking about Audrey. I never touched her! That week I spent with her, I spent in a closet. I was her prisoner! We weren't in love!"

Gosh said, "I believe you."

So who was Vicki's father, then?

Baron Mencken, but how was Gosh to know that?

"Your son was about to tell me what happened after you got lost."

"It's a long story."

"That's what Junior said."

"I mean, it's a *long* story."

Gosh said, "I'm interested."

So, obviously, were four million other people—the people who made Junior's *Honky Tonk Jungle* such a huge audio bestseller last year. And because the HTM's odyssey—his abduction by desperate mosquitoes, his long ordeal as a blood-host, his daring escape, his forbidden courtship with a tribal princess, his bitter feud with the dog people of inner Earth—is so well-known by this time, there's no point in retelling it here.

Gosh heard the tale, firsthand, though, partly in the jungle, and partly by the campfire, which burned completely out by the time the Honky Tonk Man was finished.

"And you actually prefer to keep living *here*, like *this*?" said Gosh.

Junior said, "See, Daddy, *he* thinks it's crazy, too."

The Honky Tonk Man stared at his own flat stomach for a little while, then he looked at Junior, then he got up. "You do what you want," he said. "but your mama's gonna be very upset if you leave."

"Shoot, she'll be glad to get rid of me," said Junior.

Gosh briefly watched the HTM move toward the trees, then

he scrambled to his feet. "Well, how about if you just go back for a short *visit*?" he called.

The Honky Tonk Man kept walking.

"If you expect to tap him on the head, you'd better tap now," said Junior. "Too—"

Gosh kicked at some embers.

"—late."

Gosh sat back down.

"So tell me about Wonder City," said Junior. "Are the girls pretty? Do the people ride around in rocket ships?"

"I *could've* stopped him," Gosh said out loud, but to himself.

"Does it cost a lot of money to buy a house? Does my father still have any assets, do you think? Do you think I could get at them?"

"Ma Zomba is going to be very angry with me. It'll be back to square one with her," said Gosh. "And with Vicki. Bet you she won't go blind-dancing with me *now*."

"I'd like to see a movie," said Junior. "And I'd like to see San Francisco. And the Grand Canyon. And Paris!"

Yawning, Gosh said, "Scratch Paris, Junior. You stayed away too long."

CHAPTER 44

Judging by the number of confounding changes he discovered upon his return to Wonder City, Gosh quickly came to believe that *he* had stayed away too long.

Scarcely a week had passed, yet it may as well have been a month. According to Weinstein's Revised Law of the Future, it practically *had* been. Weinstein, you remember Alf Weinstein—he was in all the newspapers, and on television quite a lot. Weinstein: the Nobel guy from MIT who'd made good cosmology out of the old saying, "Time flies."

Time flies, and flies faster as time goes by.

If Weinstein's Law *wasn't* true, then how else explain all of *this* having happened in only nine days? Gosh's American Legion barracks had been bulldozed, and on the spot now stood the concrete-block foundation, the subflooring, and the load-bearing wall of a suburban-style two-family house. Shrike had disappeared, after dissolving his media firm. The Blue Robot had been firebombed, and No-Deposit, along with all the other Tandys, sold for scrap. Del Forno was in the hospital. Julie Jeeters had straightened her hair and dyed it platinum.

Junior Tonk (as he'd decided to call himself) clapped Gosh on the shoulder and said, "You better sit down, boy. You look kind of shaky."

Gosh *felt* kind of shaky, and collapsed in a plastic visitor's chair in Del's hospital room. Julie was there. The television was playing, a late-morning soap opera. Ding. "Doctor Thompson, please come to the nurse's station." Ding. "Doctor Thompson."

Del and Julie were staring at Gosh, their mouths firm, their demeanor unfriendly.

"What're you looking at *me* for?" Gosh said. "I didn't do anything. I was in the Amazon jungle!"

"Well, it's all your fault," said Del. Both his legs were in traction, and his face was bandaged like a mummy's. "You should've known better not to tell Shrike what really happened to you."

"What?" said Gosh, jumping to his feet, ready to argue. *"What?"*

"You told him about the Jiffy. So what's he do, he suddenly decides he doesn't want to be your agent anymore, and goes to work for Ma Zomba."

Gosh sat down again.

"Boy, that lady is something *else*," said Junior. "One of these days I gotta meet her."

"Zip it up," said Gosh, and turned to Julie. "So then what?"

"So then of course Ma Zomba snatched Ira, and now she's probably making him build another Jiffy just for her. And it is *so* all your fault!" The skin below her eyes turned blotchy red.

Ira had been kidnapped three mornings ago. He'd finally decided to take driving lessons, but when the car from the Automobile Driving Institute arrived in Avenue M to pick him up for his first lesson, it was a Cadillac Caudillo. Ira had called Julie later that same day, and in a flat, slow voice told her that he wouldn't be coming home again, ever, but not to worry.

"And what happened to *you*?" Gosh asked Del.

"I went on television and told the whole story."

"You did *what*?"

"Went on television. Told the story. Spilled the beans." He jiggled his legs as best he could. "This was Ma's way of getting even. See what I get for telling the truth, for once?"

"The police are looking for her?"

"Oh, yeah," said Del. "They got arrest warrants for her and Vicki, and for Shrike, too. I don't care how great a guy he is, I hate his guts. And I'm not so crazy about yours, either, at the moment."

"Oh man," said Gosh, rubbing both palms across his scalp. It *was* all his fault. Oh man oh man. What a dumbo he was! He wondered if Ma Zomba had sent him along on that nitwit expedition just to get him out of the *way,* now that he was so powerful and stuff. "I'll find Ira," he said. "I will! Honest!" He made a fist and banged Del's bedside table.

Naturally, the whole thing collapsed, scattering tumblers, drinking straws, a plastic water jug, and caster wheels every which way.

"Nice shot, Sherlock," said Del.

But Gosh didn't hear him. He was staring at his pinky knuckle, flabbergasted.

The skin had split open, and he was bleeding a little.

He was bleeding! He'd split open his knuckle!

What th—!

CHAPTER

Coming back from Rio, Gosh had sneaked one of the expedition's ash hounds, the one named Devil, into his duffel bag, intending to give it to Del as a gift. Maybe he'd still do that, later, but for right now, he was keeping it.

He intended to use it to find Ira Jeeters. "I should get some points for this idea," he told Julie, back at the light-bulb factory.

She said nothing, still acting very cool toward him.

He shrugged and ran a Dustbuster over one of Jeeters's undershirts.

Junior Tonk had tagged along, and now was strolling around, studying the lab's electronic equipment with awe. "What's a person *do* with all this stuff?" he said. "Is this furniture?" He was dressed in blue jeans and a white T-shirt, but had insisted on going shoeless.

"You're lucky you weren't there at the Robot when the place was bombed," Gosh said to Julie.

"Yeah," she replied, clipped. Then she said, "Why would you even *think* I might've been at the Blue Robot? Huh? You think I was hanging around that place? Huh? Is that what you think? You think me and Delbert were going *out,* or something? Huh? *Huh?*"

"Forget it. I was just making a remark."

"Well, keep your remarks to yourself. And just go find my brother."

"All right, I will," said Gosh, with hurt feelings. "I will. No sweat. Don't sweat it."

"I won't."

"Good."

"Fine."

They glared at each other, Gosh waiting for her to blush or crack a winning smile. Only, this time she did neither.

"Does *everybody* have this kind of stuff in their house?" said Junior, vaulting onto a mainframe computer, then stretching out on top. "And I always thought it was uncomfortable living in a rubber tree!"

174

Gosh had some trouble mastering the ash hound, and had to refer often to the Help menu in its flank, trying endless keystroke combinations. Finally, though, he got the thing to accept Jeeters's body ash.

"What happens now?" said Julie.

"Now I just follow it."

"Well—go ahead."

Making a disgruntled face, Gosh told Junior to get a move on, if he was coming along.

As the hound was on its hydraulic way to the door, Nippy bounded in—did she ever just *walk* anyplace?—and began to bark at it.

Gosh hadn't seen Julie's pet in quite some time, and what struck him first was the weirdly bright shine to her eyes. And it wasn't his imagination, she was definitely much thicker around the middle than she used to be; she looked almost tubby.

"Stop that barking!" said Julie. "Stop it!"

She stooped and yanked on the dog's leather collar.

Nippy struggled, but couldn't break free. She *couldn't?*

Gosh frowned. "Is she—just an ordinary dog again?"

Julie nodded, then said, "How about yourself?"

"Hey, don't worry about *me*," said Gosh. "I killed a mosquito the other day with my bare hands."

CHAPTER

46

It took Devil not even two hours to lead Gosh and Junior to Ira Jeeters, and if it hadn't been for Wonder City's wicked air pollution it would've taken less than that.

The building the ash hound eventually stopped at was only a dozen or so blocks west of Avenue M, a two-story windowless cube of corrugated steel on Taxes Boulevard. The modest sign in front said "EMZEE LTD. NO INQUIRIES."

"I don't see any bell," said Gosh.

"I don't see any *door*," said Junior, and when Gosh realized that the jungle boy was right, that there *was* no door, he felt pretty stupid for not having noticed that himself. He wandered around the building. No windows, no entrances. He stood on the pavement, scratching his head.

Immediately next to Emzee Ltd. was a real ozone scraper, the staggeringly high Uneeda Insurance building, and since it was lunchtime, the plaza was thick with junior executives and secretaries and mailroom people, everybody out sunning themselves. A number of them were openly watching Junior and Gosh, their attentions having been piqued originally by the arrival of an ash hound, not something you saw every day in the big city.

A young brunette woman dressed in a pinstriped suit and a conservative necktie folded up her sun reflector and came over to Gosh. "I think the only way to get in there is underground," she said, trying to be helpful. "There must be a tunnel from one of the other buildings around here." Although she was speaking to Gosh, she was eyeing Junior, brazenly. "Or you can try the roof, I suppose, if you can find a ladder." She pressed her lips together briefly, to indicate that she was now being facetious. Then she said, "I haven't seen hair so long on a guy in my life."

"He's been living in the jungle," said Gosh, starting to unbutton his shirt.

"Really? I like it."

Junior said, "You can talk to me, girl, I speak English."

"Girl? *Girl?*" The businesswoman laughed, astonished and charmed. "*I'll* say he's been in the jungle!"

Gosh nodded, and kicked off his sneakers, so that he could get his legs out of his pants. Then he put his sneakers back on.

Junior studied Gosh's neat uniform, and wanted to know, "Does *everybody* wear that kind of thing under their clothes?"

"Where am I going to put this stuff?" Gosh said, looking around for a place to stash his shirt and pants.

"I'll hold it." It was Julie Jeeters.

"I *thought* I saw you following us," said Gosh, beginning to grin. "And could you kind of keep an eye on the ash hound for me, too?"

Julie maintained her stone face, but took Gosh's street clothes. "It's my lot in life," she said to the businesswoman.

"What is?"

"Doing favors for other people."

"Does it make you happy?"

"Hardy har-har."

Gosh had turned around and was looking up the front of the steel cube.

"You want me to go witchoo?" said Junior.

"How're you going to get to the roof?"

"Climb, how else? How're *you* gonna do it, fly?"

And Gosh said, "Yeah."

CHAPTER

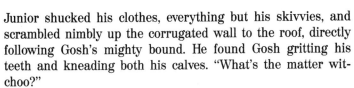

Junior shucked his clothes, everything but his skivvies, and scrambled nimbly up the corrugated wall to the roof, directly following Gosh's mighty bound. He found Gosh gritting his teeth and kneading both his calves. "What's the matter wit-choo?"

"I think I pulled something. Like a tendon, or something."

"I'm not surprised. How'd you jump like that?"

"It's all breaking down, I'm losing it!"

"Losing what?" said Junior, shifting from one foot to the other, because the steel roof was burning hot.

Gosh was sitting on the roof, and felt a slight warmth through the leotard. "I'm really losing it," he said, his voice hollow in his ringing ears.

"Yeah, and I'm getting blisters. Let's *do* something."

So Gosh stood up and wrenched the skylight out of its frame, which left his arms feeling like two wet noodles, absolutely useless.

Then he and Junior dropped into a daisy chain of armed zombies.

CHAPTER

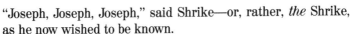

"Joseph, Joseph, Joseph," said Shrike—or, rather, *the* Shrike, as he now wished to be known.

Gosh's arms hung lifelessly at his sides, and he was limping around, trying to work a charley horse out of one leg.

Junior was sitting dejectedly on the carpet, his legs drawn up to his chest. He had his chin tucked against a shoulder, and was cleaning a flesh wound with his tongue. The zombies had worked him over pretty good. They'd roughed Gosh up, too—bloodied his lip, blackened both his eyes—but they hadn't been quite as thorough with him as they'd been with Junior. While vulnerable again, Gosh's skin was still preternaturally solid and hard. It *hurt* to beat him.

They'd dragged them both into an empty, carpeted office, and locked them in.

"I thought you told me you could bop somebody cold with just a little tap," Junior had said, crawling into a corner on all fours.

And Gosh had said, "Just shut up, all right?"

Twenty minutes later, the Shrike had walked in wearing a shiny black jumpsuit. At first, Gosh hadn't recognized him. He'd had cosmetic surgery on his face, and the vicious-looking bird beak grafted to his nose changed his whole appearance. Also, his fingers bore talons. "What're *you* supposed to be?" said Gosh, ogling the beak, the rasorial claws, and the jumpsuit.

"The Shrike! *The* Shrike. You know about shrikes, Joseph? They're, like, these predatory birds that impale their prey on thorns or fences. Cool, huh? Ma told me all about them. And *I* always thought it was just my name!"

Gosh said, "You're really . . . you're really a lousy—"

"Now, now, Joseph," said the Shrike, waggling a claw.

"Oh, come on! I mean, I like you a lot and all, and you're a good guy and all, but—you betrayed me!"

"All right, so I did. So I did. But you have to understand, that media consulting just wasn't for me, you know? It was stifling my creative juices! But now I think I've finally found the one thing I can excel at. I think crime is really where I'm going to come into my own. Especially once I've been through the Jiffy."

"Well, I wish you the best of luck," said Gosh, and he couldn't, he absolutely *could not believe* what he was saying. Shrike—*the* Shrike—really *did* have the most dangerous pheromones on planet Earth.

"We didn't expect you back for another few weeks, at least," the Shrike said.

"We couldn't find the Honky Tonk Man."

"You mustn't've looked very hard."

"It was too hot."

The Shrike laughed. "And who's this funny little fella?" he said, meaning Junior, of course.

"Oh, just some kid we picked up on the river. He was raised by hyenas."

"I didn't know there were hyenas in Brazil."

Gosh rolled his eyes, then tried to sit down on the floor, but the charley horse came right back, zing!

"So the Jiffy treatment isn't permanent, I see," said the Shrike.

"Apparently not."

The Shrike considered for a long moment, then shrugged. "The gizmo might prove more valuable that way," he said. "If we decide to market it as a service, I mean. Because we'd get repeat business. On the other hand, if we use it to just, you know, become superpowered criminals, it might be a real drag, having to jump back into it every month and a half."

"Yeah, it might," Gosh agreed.

The Shrike gave half a shrug. "I'll have to talk things over with Ma and Vicki." He brought out chewing gum—from one of the many, many pockets in his jumpsuit—took a stick, then offered the pack to Gosh, who declined it. "You hungry? You want me to send somebody up with a sandwich? A bottle of soda?"

"Skip it," said Gosh. "By the way, what happened to my house? Everything I owned was in there."

"I sold it."

"What?"

"I said, I sold it. Right after I got out of public relations, I went into the realty business for a day or two."

"You sold the barracks?"

"I had to share my commission with a licensed broker, but, still, I walked away with ninety-seven thousand dollars. It's a seller's market these days, believe me."

"Where's my furniture? What about all my *things*?"

"I really don't know. I guess—gee, I don't have any *idea* what might've happened to them. Did you talk to the builder?"

"Go away, Shrike," said Gosh, squeezing his face between his hands. "Just leave."

"Hey, Joseph, don't get so upset. What did you have? A lot of junk. The refrigerator wasn't even worth two thousand bucks."

"Hey," called Junior, "you ever gonna let us out of here?"

The Shrike smiled amiably and gave Junior a helping hand to his feet. Then, really laying on the scent, he said, "Well, I don't think we can do that. We'll probably turn you both into zombies. Enslave you guys for, like, the rest of your lives."

"Gee, thanks," said Junior, sincerely. "You're good people, I could tell."

Through the floor, Gosh felt strong vibrations, and when he pulled up an edge of beige carpeting and pressed his ear to the parquet, he could hear human voices, below.

They'd been locked up for over an hour now. Gosh was

still nervous, but, strangely enough, he was also beginning to feel insulted, he supposed for being treated like a common trespasser instead of as a real threat. He had to lose his powers today, of all days! Beautiful.

Junior had fallen into mopish lethargy again once the Shrike had gone.

Watching Gosh flip the carpet back into place, he said, "I don't *want* to be a zombie! Why'd I sound so grateful? Shoot!"

"He has that effect on everybody."

"Who does? The Shrike?"

Gosh nodded, thinking, The Shrike! What a clown that guy is.

"Listen, Junior. Let's get out of here. Let's think of something and get out of here."

"I'm witchoo. I don't wanna be no zombie! From a monkey to a zombie's not exactly what I had in mind."

"Me, either," said Gosh, "me, either."

Literally, Gosh used his head to escape.

His arms were no longer anything to write home about, and neither were his legs (he tried both), but his head, of all things, was still fairly hard, so he batted it against the door, just above the knob, and after three or four loud clunks, it flew open. That miraculous feat left Gosh feeling more than a little punchy, though, and he staggered so badly, threatening to fall down, that Junior had to take his elbow. "Man, you *really* are losing it. Whatever it was you had."

Gosh's pupils had dilated to gumdrops, and his scalp was bleeding, matting his hair. He'd just given himself a serious concussion. Great! Just wonderful! What a headache! Was he going to throw up?

"How're we gonna get outta here?" Junior asked. "Same way we got in?"

"I'm going down to the first floor," Gosh replied. He blinked rapidly, then stared at Junior, all of a sudden terribly confused. Who *was* this long-haired, practically naked, pesty kid? "I . . . I have superpowers. I'm going to, to, um, fix everything. Make everything right. Fix everything. This is my—this is what I *do* for a living."

"Hey, guy, I think what you're losing right now are your marbles. We gotta get *outta* here. Not go downstairs. I should never've come in witchoo."

Gosh frowned, moistened his lips—man, was his mouth as dry as dust—and set off limping down the hallway. Junior made a throaty sound of disgust, but finally went after him, and prevented Gosh from just turning the corner as if he were on his way to the neighborhood delicatessen for a quart of milk. When Junior peeked around into the adjacent corridor, he immediately pulled back. "There's a bunch of those guys that beat us up, and they're coming this way. Move," he whispered, "move!" He kept shoving Gosh, and trying every doorknob they passed. Finally, they slipped through a door just as the zombies came into sight.

It was a room full of color monitors; there must've been, oh, three dozen or more, Zeniths, embedded in the walls. Instantly fascinated, Junior sank into a Leatherette chair, his attention flicking from screen to screen, from a bank vault to a boardroom to the Oval Office in the White House, where the President of the United States, alone, could be seen working out with hand weights.

Junior laughed, watching the zombie guards discover the empty office where he and Gosh had been held prisoner, and his eyes widened when, on another monitor, he spotted that guy, the Shrike, talking to a fat lady and a pretty young woman, and he frowned darkly as he saw Julie Jeeters being dragged down a long tunnel by a couple of thugs. And then, on a monitor mounted just above his head, he watched himself look surprised as he and Joe Gosh were jumped from behind and clubbed to their knees.

Gosh kept squeezing his eyes shut, then opening them again suddenly, trying to reduce the number of Ma Zombas, Julies, Vickis, Iras, Juniors, and Shrikes crowding his brown, watery vision.

When he'd been hustled roughly into the makeshift laboratory, his sore arms tied behind his back, he'd seen three or four of everybody. His strategy was working, though, because now there were only two or three of each. His stomach was upset and his headache was an absolute killer, but he was determined not to embarrass himself in front of the whole gang by becoming ill or passing out.

"I always knew you were a real nobody at heart, Joe Gosh," said Ma Zomba in triplicate.

"Wow," muttered Junior under his breath, "no *wonder* Daddy wouldn't give her a tumble. She's *mean*."

"*What* did you say?" said Ma, turning to him swiftly.

"Nothing, ma'am."

"And who are you, anyhow?"

"Nobody, ma'am, just the hyena boy," he replied, lowering his head and beginning to hum along with the recorded music—naturally another song by the Honky Tonk Man—that was playing on a tape deck. "Are You Lonesome Tonight."

With Ma's attention diverted from him, Gosh looked around, at a couple of Ira Jeeters squatted by a pair of brand-new Jiffys and plugging in jacks. Three Julies were trying to talk to both Iras, but none of them could get the two geniuses' attention. Gosh shook his head, and wished that his hands were free, so he could remove his stupid goggles and knuckle his eye sockets. This multiple-vision stuff was driving him crazy.

The Iras stood up, looked at the Ma Zombas, and said, "Ready to rip, boss."

"Oh, can I go first?" said the Vickis. They were sitting on a little couch with the Shrikes, carefully applying red lacquer to many talons. "Can I? I want to go first."

"Before *anybody* goes in that thing, we run a little test, all right with you, professor?"

"Anything you want, boss," Jeeters and Jeeters-prime replied obsequiously.

Ma, and Ma and Ma, nodded, then strode up to Gosh. He shut his eyes again, but this time he kept them shut. But she didn't try to zombify him, she merely yanked the aviator glasses off his head. "Put these through," she told Jeeters. "And *this* receiver better *receive,* or you'll be out mugging priests and nuns seven days a week."

"Oh, it'll receive," said Ira, "it'll receive. All the glitches are—"

"Just show me," said Ma, tossing him the goggles.

As Jeeters set them inside the transmission stall, Gosh struggled with his bonds, and ground his teeth so hard that several back cavities throbbed. But hooray! some rope fibers gave. He tried not to fidget a lot, but needn't have worried about attracting attention. Everybody, even Julie (who'd been nabbed, by the way, when she'd tried to telephone the police from the lobby of the Uneeda building), was absorbed in watching Jeeters do his wizardry at the Jiffy control panel.

As the goggles vanished, the Honky Tonk Man was singing "Mama's Hungry Eyes."

About thirty seconds later, during the first verse of "The Wild Side of Life," the goggles reappeared across the room in the receiving stall.

"See, boss,?" said Jeeters. "What'd I tell you? Perfecto!"

"So—now me first!" said Vicki Zomba, propelling herself off the sofa and practically running to the transmitter. Julie stuck out a foot to trip her, but retracted it in cowardice at the last possible moment. Vicki ensconced herself in the Jiffy. "Okay," she said, "ready!"

"Get out of there, you selfish nit," said Ma. *"I'm* going first."

"Oh, no you're not! I don't *trust* you!"

"Your own *mother?*" said Ma, ingenuously shocked. "You don't trust your own mother?"

Vicki snorted, as if the question were too ludicrous for a reply, and stayed put.

Ma tramped over to the Jiffy. "You get out of there right this minute, young lady, or I'll *make* you get out."

"Just try it, you old, you old—*hypnotist!* Two-bit hypnotist!"

"Ladies, ladies," said the Shrike, "let's not ruin a novel experience with this petty bickering." He stood up and blew on his wet talons. "If you don't mind, *I'll* go first."

"Like heck you will," said Ma Zomba, turning to face him, and squinting.

The Shrike blinked, but before he went completely under

her spell, he paddled his hands in front of his chest, wafting hormonal scents at her.

And the upshot of all this was, they turned as mutually deferential as Alphonse and Gaston: "Oh, I guess you should go first," said the Shrike. "No, please," said Ma, "you go, I insist."

"Well, then *I'll* go, and that'll settle it," said Vicki.

But neither Ma nor the Shrike would agree to *that*.

It was a complete stalemate, until Junior suggested, "Why don't you all go *together*? It looks like there's enough room." He turned to Gosh and muttered, "And once they're gone, we're outta here, right?"

Gosh nodded, and snapped more rope.

If the consequences of all this weren't so dire (imagine a superpowered Ma Zomba; why, she could conquer the world!), it would've been a riot, seeing Vicki, the Shrike, and the Queen of Crime trying to squeeze into that Jeeter Jiffy, stepping on each other's feet, avoiding elbows, shifting around to get more comfortable. Once they were fitted in as well as they'd ever be, Ma said, "Make sure nobody leaves," to the zombie guards who'd brought Julie, Gosh, and Junior into the lab.

"Well, there goes *my* big idea," said Junior with a moan of chagrin.

"Stoke the boiler, Mr. Engineer," the Shrike called to Jeeters, "and let's get this train on down the track."

Jeeters, however, wasn't taking orders from anyone except Ma Zomba. He waited for her curt nod before flipping switches and typing up an alphanumerical storm. And as the unholy trio faded gradually from view—the Shrike waving like a politician accepting his party's nomination for high office, Ma scowling, and Vicki brushing a lick of hair off her forehead—the Honky Tonk Man's famous baritone filled the air, singing "Green, Green Grass of Home."

Then Gosh grunted, and burst the last of his bonds. First thing he did was rub his eyes.

The zombies, who were all staring like cows at the empty receiving stall, didn't notice right away that Gosh was free. But they certainly noticed when, all at once, he plowed through them, flinging them aside like rag effigies. Planting himself in front of the stall, he spread his arms and gripped both sides, intending to wrench it from its base and throw it—somewhere, anywhere, just wreck it. Strand those suckers in the blue desert.

But who was he kidding? He'd lost all his cool powers, he was a nobody again, just another slob, a debtor with no visible means of support. He couldn't destroy a toaster, much less a matter transmitter!

The zombies all leapt on his back, one right on top of the other, like a pack of cub scouts playing Johnny, Ride a White Horse, and Gosh tottered, staggered, bit somebody's thumb, then somebody's forearm, than a wrist, a knuckle, another thumb.

Behind him, he heard Ira Jeeters exclaim, "They're coming through—I see them!"

Directly in front of Gosh now, only a foot away, Ma Zomba's face shimmered, then Vicki's did. With a tremendous effort, Gosh heaved the zombies off his back, and, as veins bulged in his forehead, he lifted the Jiffy, popping its cables and creating a gale of sparks. For an instant, he thought he saw the Shrike's beaky face flicker in the air.

Gosh raised the stall above his head, as he himself was forced to his knees, his miraculous burst of strength draining fast. With one last, exhausting effort, he heaved the new, improved Jiffy across the room, where it smashed against a wall and was utterly demolished.

Jeeters screamed in anguish, "Not again! Gosh, I'm going to sue your butt off!"

"Ira!" shouted Julie. "You're your old self again!" And she hugged him around the neck while he grumbled and stamped his feet.

Meanwhile, the other zombies were all behaving as if they'd just woken up from a long snooze—yawning and

stretching and scraping their coated tongues with their front teeth. The lot of them were mystified; several of them burst into tears, convinced that they'd died and that this place was some sort of anteroom to the afterlife. Three or four of them ran up to Gosh, begging him for an *explanation*, but he didn't respond. He was staring in disbelief at the Jiffy wreckage.

How did I do *that*? he thought. Then he looked at his hands. They were red and astonishingly sore, and nicked with tiny cuts. If he wasn't a superman any longer, how the *heck* did he manage *that*? Adrenaline? Another victory for the common man? There's a hero born every second? Something like that. A person is a big solid elevation of a cell. Ain't it great, aren't we swell?

Beaming, Gosh folded his arms across his chest.

Well done! he congratulated himself. Well *done*, you big nobody!

But his gloating was cut short by Junior's trebled yelp.

Something was happening to the Jiffy's transmitter! With a great whoosh! it began spewing blue sand into the laboratory, blinding, stinging vortices of the stuff. And along with the sand came sand hearts, screeching like sonar. Julie shouted for Ira to turn off the Jiffy, turn it *off* (Gosh could hear her, not see her), and Ira shouted back, "I can't, it won't *turn* off!" Swell. Terrific. Par for the course.

As the storm turned ever more violent, and as more and more hearts came spinning into our funny old dimension, Gosh blundered around, trying to locate the door. Suddenly, Junior grabbed his wrist. "Somebody's pulling me," he said, "so just hold on."

Gosh did as he was told, joining the conga line to freedom, and while he was pulled along, he picked up a former zombie, who picked up another former zombie, and so on. They all stumbled into another room, with the sand blowing in after them, but there, at least, Gosh could open his eyes and see again. He saw Junior clutching Ira's shorttail, Ira gripping Julie's forearm with both hands. Julie was leading the way, dragging everyone into a corridor, then through a doorway and into a low tunnel that connected the corrugated box with the Uneeda Building.

Moments later, panting and sweating, they burst through the back wall of a telephone booth and spilled out the folding door into the lobby, startling the blind guy in the magazine kiosk.

THE LAST CHAPTER

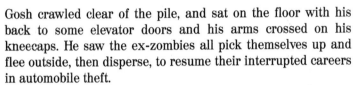

Gosh crawled clear of the pile, and sat on the floor with his back to some elevator doors and his arms crossed on his kneecaps. He saw the ex-zombies all pick themselves up and flee outside, then disperse, to resume their interrupted careers in automobile theft.

While Gosh ran a pinky tip around the inner rim of an ear, flicking out blue grit, he noticed that Junior Tonk had become engaged in conversation with that brunette businesswoman from before. Junior said something, and she smiled, then handed him back his pants and shirt, which she'd been holding onto for him since he'd followed Gosh to the roof. (Her name, incidentally, was Ruth Dancer, and she was director of marketing for Alternate World Press, a major publishing company.) As Gosh looked dully on, she escorted the jungle boy over to the bank of elevators. Junior reached down and shook Gosh's hand. "This pretty lady, here, says she's gonna make me rich," he said.

Gosh nodded.

An elevator arrived, and Gosh nearly fell into it when the doors opened. He stood up and watched Junior and Ruth Dancer step inside. The operator asked Gosh, "Going up?"

He smiled and shook his head no.

The doors began to close, and Junior waved, then blurted suddenly to Gosh, "What's an auto*bog*raphy, anyhow?"

Then he was gone.

On the opposite side of the lobby, Ira Jeeters was bossing Julie around once more, gesturing for her to brush sand off his shoulders.

"If you hadn't always complained about me not having a driver's license, this wouldn't've happened, Juliet."

"Oh, dry up," she said.

Gosh stepped back into the phone booth and slammed the trick wall completely shut, then he heaved a great sigh—of what? tiredness? disappointment? satisfaction? all three, really—and walked across the lobby and out the revolving doors.

There was a huge crowd gathered in Taxes Boulevard now, a couple hundred citizens watching the once-in-a-lifetime phenomenon happening above the roof of Emzee Ltd. It was a blue tornado, a perfect meteorological funnel, and as it spun furiously, it began to suck up the corrugated cube, while at the same time centrifugally flinging sand hearts in every direction. Police were arriving, and zoo personnel with nets.

Gosh stayed to watch the tornado expend its energy and fizzle out till finally there was nothing next door to the Uneeda Building but a large, empty blue beach.

Could this really be the end of Ma Zomba?

Probably not.

"Your clothes."

Gosh turned to find Julie Jeeters standing beside him, pulling his shirt and jeans from her shoulder bag.

"Thanks," he said, avoiding her eyes. "Thanks a lot."

"You're welcome," she said. Then she said, "I'm smiling, in case you're interested."

At last, he summoned up the nerve to look at her directly, and, indeed, she was smiling.

"Well—thanks again," he said, taking his stuff from her. He made some liquidy mouth noise, racking his brain for something to say next. She waited, patiently. "You must think I'm a pretty big jerk, all in all," he finally said, and put on his pants.

She said, "Yeah, I guess."

Gosh frowned. "But I just, you know, was trying to find something *interesting* to do with my life." He shrugged, and buttoned his shirt.

"Maybe you should've read some matchbooks. You ever think of being a truck driver? Or a CPA?"

Gosh set his teeth, and looked away, at a couple of zoo men, and at Devil the ash hound, all three of them scrambling across the avenue after a fleet heart. "You're making fun of me," he said.

"I am."

"I deserve it."

"You do. A guy who'd fall for that Vicki person deserves whatever he gets."

"What, you didn't think she was at least *pretty*?"

"I'm still smiling, Gosh. See? Don't press your luck."

Gosh shrugged and fell silent. Half a minute later, he said, "Well . . ."

"Well, what?"

"Well—I don't *know* what!" he said hoarsely. Then it all hit him, all of a sudden, like a ton of dishes: ai, yi, yi! What's going to happen to me *now*? He realized he was shaking. "Oh, man, Julie, I'm *really* up the creek! I'm broke, they're probably going to send me to *Mars,* my house is *gone,* my furniture is gone, my *clothes* are gone! My blues records! My pinball machine! And Del won't *talk* to me. Worse than that, he probably won't *lend* me any more money, either." He pushed his fingers through his hair. "But worst of *all*—worst of all, I'm just an ordinary . . . Joe again. I'm aching all over." .

"My hero," she said.

"Stop teasing, I feel crummy enough."

"Who's teasing?" she said, hooking her arm through Gosh's. "When you picked up the Jiffy and threw it? I was very impressed."

"Yeah?"

"Very," she replied, as they started walking toward the corner.

There was a lottery machine there, and Gosh paused to look at it longingly.

"The odds," said Julie, "are ten zillion to one."

"That bad?"

She nodded. "But don't worry," she said, "I won't let them send you to Mars."

"You won't?"

"It'll all work out," she said. "We'll think of something."

"*We* will?"

She leaned over and kissed him on the cheek, and as they were crossing the boulevard, against the light, Gosh, on a sudden impulse, closed his eyes. Julie followed suit, and, reckless, they blind-danced together in midday traffic. Waltzed across Taxes, and made it safely to the opposite curb.

"Did you peek?" Julie asked him.

"Nope. Did you?"

She smiled serenely.

Ira Jeeters burst out of the Uneeda Building and called after them from the plaza. "Hey! Hey, Julie, did you bring the car? Julie! Hey! I need a lift home!"

But she didn't look back, and neither did Joe Gosh, and as Del Forno would phrase it several months later once he'd resumed storytelling at his brand-new club, the Blue Heart, "They lived happily, and otherwise, ever after, and did lots of really neat stuff together, no lie, but I don't have the time to tell you *everything*. What do you *want* for a lousy hundred-dollar cover charge, the *moon*? Thank you, ladies and gentlemen, and good night."